Taryn Leigh Taylor likes dinosaurs, bridges and space—both personal and the final frontier variety. She shamelessly indulges in clichés, most notably her Starbucks addiction: grande six-pump, whole milk, no water, chai tea latte—aka 'the usual'—her shoe hoard (*I can stop any time I... Ooh! These are pretty!*) and her penchant for falling in lust with fictional men with great abs. She also really loves books, which was what sent her down the crazy path of writing in the first place. Want to be virtual friends? Check out tarynleightaylor.com, Facebook.com/tarynltaylor1 and Twitter, @tarynltaylor.

If you liked *Forbidden Pleasure*, why not try

Close to the Edge by Zara Cox
Beddable Billionaire by Alexx Andria
Getting Lucky by Avril Tremayne

Discover more at millsandboon.co.uk

FORBIDDEN
PLEASURE

TARYN LEIGH TAYLOR

MILLS & BOON

First Published in Great Britain 2018
by Mills & Boon, an imprint of HarperCollins*Publishers*
1 London Bridge Street, London, SE1 9GF

© 2018 Taryn Leigh Taylor

ISBN: 978-0-263-93231-7

MIX
Paper from
responsible sources
FSC® C007454

Printed and bound in Spain
by CPI, Barcelona

For Xtal—I can't thank you enough for everything you do, most notably putting up with me during the writing process. No jokes this time, just the stone-cold truth.

And for Jo—Thanks for making this period of great transition so easy and seamless. It's been a pleasure working with you. (Except on the nights our teams face off against each other and I'm forced to despise you on principle. But all the rest of the time it's been great!)

CHAPTER ONE

EMMA MATHISON WAS ready to get wild.

She reached up and undid the top button of her blouse.

Well, at least as wild as she could get for someone who was still in the office at eight o'clock on a Friday night.

At some point during the last three years, it had become the status quo—dinner at her desk, working until eight or nine, home to bed, and returning bright and early in the morning to do it all again. Emma couldn't remember the last time she'd had plans. With a sigh, she leaned forward over the sink, inspecting herself in the harsh fluorescent lighting.

She barely recognized the professional-looking woman in the mirror. Blond chignon, subdued makeup, conservative blouse. The result of years spent focused everywhere but on herself—fighting to keep it together both financially and emotionally as Alzheimer's stripped her beautiful, vivacious, hardworking mother of her memories, her personality and finally her life.

Emma touched her thumb to the simple silver band

she wore on the middle finger of her right hand. Ana Petrović-Mathison's most prized possession—her wedding ring. The loss was still a gut punch, but she made herself breathe through it. Her mother had worn it as a tribute to a life well-lived. Emma wore it now as a warning that life was short.

Fourteen-hour workdays that barely made a dent in the pile of medical bills. A roster of acquaintances on Facebook, but no real friends. A tiny apartment where no one waited to welcome her home. It scared Emma, the realization that if she suffered the same fate as her mother, if Alzheimer's came for her one day, she had no memories to lose.

But there was still time to change that, to reclaim the woman she'd been before hospitals and hopelessness and grief had worn her down to a meek, biddable shell of her former self.

Starting now.

She tugged the bobby pins from her hair, shaking it out so it fell in loose waves down her back. Dropping the pins into her secondhand Michael Kors tote, she pulled out a tube of red lipstick. It had been an impulse purchase, the opposite of the pinks and nudes she usually opted for, but like the sexy lingerie hiding beneath her staid blouse and demure pencil skirt, it had been carefully chosen to keep her courage up.

And yeah, she thought, painting her lips ruby red before tucking the lipstick away, maybe the bathroom at Whitfield Industries was not the most auspicious place to launch her emancipation, but if she'd learned one thing over the last three years, it was that life wasn't perfect.

If you waited for the stars to align, you missed out.

To that end, she readjusted her boobs to get every dollar's worth of "lift and separate" out of her extravagantly priced bra and gave herself a final once-over.

With a deep breath, Emma stared at the daring, crimson-lipped woman reflecting back at her. The one who was about to go and seduce her boss.

"Time to make some memories," she told her reflection.

She undid two more buttons on her blouse, grabbed her bag from the edge of the sink and then strode across the tiled floor with visions of the kick-ass, take-no-prisoners life she planned to live from here on out.

Despite her bathroom bravado, her pace slowed the closer she got to her target. Ignoring the sudden rush of nerves, Emma lifted her chin. "Do not chicken out now." She said the words aloud, half admonishment, half plea. Then, with a deep, steadying breath, she forced herself to turn the corner and the object of all her lusty fantasies came into view.

Max Whitfield.

It was often said that the CEO of Whitfield Industries was as handsome as he was controlled. Mostly, Emma had taught herself to ignore it, to focus on work. But tonight, standing outside the glass wall of his office for the last time, she let herself notice everything about him.

He was tirelessly poring over the files on his desk. His charcoal-gray jacket hung on the back of his chair, and his shirtsleeves were rolled up his tanned forearms. He'd loosened his red silk tie enough to pop the top button of his collar. Behind him, the lights of Los Angeles twinkled like fallen stars, but he kept his head down and his back to the million-dollar view. His modern, masculine office was lit only by his desk lamp and his computer screen, his preferred lighting scheme once the sun had set.

Max had always reminded her of a panther—beautiful and predatory and not to be underestimated. It wasn't just his ebony hair and amber eyes, but the way he moved, lithe and graceful. Purposeful. No wasted movement. The constant threat of danger, even in repose.

He was the kind of man who made a woman wonder—when she unwrapped him, would she find that slick, urbane control went all the way to the core, or did it hide something more dangerous, something desperate to be unleashed?

In her fantasies, she vacillated between the two extremes—sometimes imagining him as a fiery, insatiable lover, sometimes ice-cold and bossy, controlled throughout.

And tonight, she intended to find out which version of Max was real.

She set her tote on his admin assistant's desk—Sherri had left over an hour ago—and pulled out her employment contract. *Here goes nothing.* Squaring her shoulders, she stepped forward.

Max looked up sharply when she knocked, but the tightness in his jaw faded when he recognized her, and he motioned for her to enter. With a glance at his watch, he added, "I didn't realize it was so late. What can I do for you, Emma?"

She covered her disappointment at his lack of re-action to her new look with a smile she hoped was more come-hither than professional.

His desk wasn't ornate—the clean, simple lines of black onyx had always struck Emma as sleek and powerful, like the man who sat behind it. On a usual day, this would be the point where he launched into a rapid-fire series of orders, but tonight he said nothing, regarding her with the infamous poker face that Emma knew hid all manner of secrets.

She was careful not to let her hands shake as she set the contract on top of the files in front of him.

He ignored it, didn't even glance down. Just stared at her from across the expanse of his desk, hypnotic golden eyes boring into hers with the intensity she'd come to associate with him. Max Whitfield didn't do anything halfway.

"You didn't sign it."

It wasn't a question.

She didn't ask how he knew.

Max hadn't taken his family's scandal-ridden company from the brink of bankruptcy to a tech juggernaut within the span of five years by not knowing how to read people.

Only then did she realize she'd given herself away and was absently twisting the plain silver band on her middle finger. She dropped her hands and lifted her chin.

"So you're really going through with this?"

"If by *this*, you mean quitting, then yes. I'm really going through with this." Emma pushed a small metal statue of a horse's head with a mane of flames out of the way so she could perch a hip on the corner of his desk before she crossed her left leg over her right. It was a bold move, not one she'd ever made before, but this was a now-or-never situation—and she was Team Now, all the way. At least until he cocked an eyebrow at the liberty she'd just taken.

Her heart thudded in slow, thick beats as he trailed his imperious gaze down her body and let it linger for a moment too long on her knee, making her excruciatingly aware of how far her dress had slid up her thigh when she'd sat.

God, if having his eyes on her could make her feel this good, she couldn't wait to get his hands on her.

She waited patiently until he'd looked his fill and flicked his attention back to her face.

The raw power of him made Emma's skin hum with potential, but she faced down the electricity's source. Max didn't respect cowards. He lived in a world of high-stakes negotiations where death was preferable to shows of weakness.

"I don't know what more I can say."

"That's easy," Max countered, leaning back in his chair. "Say you'll stay."

The statement hung between them, suspended in air so thick it brushed against her skin and left goose bumps in its wake. They'd always had chemistry. Since the first time they'd laid eyes on one another. And with the same sardonic expression on his face as he wore now, he'd given her the research and development job she'd so brazenly demanded. In the space of a handshake, the sexual awareness bubbling between them had been leashed, muzzled and banished by unspoken agreement to the dungeon of professionalism.

But ever since she'd handed in her notice three weeks ago, and he'd countered with the very generous terms outlined in the unsigned contract she'd just placed on his desk, the sensual beast had awoken, prowling in the shadows, growing bolder, encroaching more often and more forcefully as their time together drew to an end. And tonight, she was going to let it loose.

Emma didn't move. And this time she would not speak first.

There was a note of respect in his voice when he conceded. "What will it take?"

"I'm sorry?"

"How much? Name your price."

It was as close to begging as she'd ever heard him get. She didn't like the answering flutter in her chest that made her want to stay. Max had a way of taking control, and she couldn't afford to let him. Not tonight.

"This isn't a negotiation. I don't have a price."

Max steepled his fingers, looking like every titan of industry in every anti-capitalist movie ever made. "*Everyone* has a price."

Her answering laugh was tinged with scorn. "Really, Max? Resorting to tired clichés already? I'd always credited you with more stamina than that."

The slow grin that dawned across his handsome features stirred something deep and primal in her belly, a silent refutation of her verbal jab that let her know that he could more than provide *whatever* she

needed for as long as she needed it. It was a rare sm[...]
for him, not the feral one he used for business, b[...]
the charming one that slipped out sometimes wh[...]
he was genuinely amused.

"What can I say? I have a deep appreciation [...]
the classics." Max dropped his hands, then sat f[...]
ward in his chair. "Now, get off my desk. You do[...]
work here anymore."

Emma had already followed the command befo[...]
she realized she'd done it. *Dammit.* No retreat, she [...]
minded herself, straightening the seams of her bla[...]
pencil skirt, wishing the slit was a little more d[...]
ing, achingly aware of the garters beneath. Igno[...]
ing the implied dismissal, she crossed her arms ov[...]
her chest, taking care to enhance her cleavage as s[...]
did so. "You're right. So maybe you should pour n[...]
a drink. We can toast the end of our working re[...]
tionship."

Oh God. Had she just said that?

He raised a contemplative eyebrow.

It was hard to breathe.

Without a word, he stood in that dangerous[...]
graceful way he had and walked over to the sid[...]
board near the window. Her heart gave a funny lit[...]
lurch at the realization it was the last time she w[...]
going to see him.

She allowed her gaze to linger a moment, to f[...]
the height and breadth of him in her mind. The qu[...]
authority of him as, with quick, efficient movemen[...]
Max pulled the stopper from the crystal decanter a[...]
poured a drink.

Then he poured another, which caused a cor[...]

pletely different kind of lurch, this one much, much lower than her heart.

This was going to happen.

Emma's palms prickled as he grabbed both glasses and joined her in front of his desk. The fact that he stood about a foot closer than he'd ever stood before was not lost on her. She accepted the drink he held out to her, her skin slick against the expensive crystal.

Max regarded her for a moment, his expression unreadable, before he raised his glass. "To whatever comes next."

His voice was deep, rich and more intoxicating than the premium liquor he'd handed her.

She clinked her glass to his and joined him in a sip of his preferred single malt Scotch.

The liquid was smooth and strong as it slipped over her tongue.

"Tell me it's not Kearney."

"What?"

"Tell me you're not leaving to work for that son of a bitch."

Emma was oddly touched by the surly order that namechecked his most hated rival, the CEO of Cybercore. In Max-speak, that might be as close as she would ever get to "It's been nice working with you." Not that she was fishing for compliments.

"Why would you think that?" she asked, taking another sip.

"Because business is war. You have to take what you want. And Liam Kearney has a long history of taking what's mine."

Emma choked on her mouthful of Scotch.

Surely he hadn't meant...

She glanced up at his stern, handsome face, but his eyes were shuttered, focused on the liquid swirling in the glass thanks to a practiced flick of his wrist, like he was lost in an unpleasant memory.

Her voice was soft when she finally spoke, and despite her better judgment, held the reverence of a vow. "I'm not going to work for that son of a bitch."

Emma was vindicated by the twitch of his lips that betrayed, if not outright relief, at least mild amusement, though she wasn't sure if it was at the solemnness of her response or at himself for stooping to ask the question. "Drink your Scotch, Emma."

It sounded almost like a warning. She stared at the contents of her glass. "We've never had a drink together before." The words were unnecessary, obvious, but she couldn't stop them anymore than she could stop her gaze from lifting to his.

If she hadn't spent the last three years working with him, day in and day out, she might have missed the tick in his jaw, the subtle darkening of his eyes.

"You've never not worked for me before," he countered, raising the glass to his lips.

Heat flared in her belly, incinerating the oxygen and making it hard to breathe. Her skin buzzed at the change in the atmosphere.

She fortified herself with another sip of the amber liquid that was as heady and intoxicating as the look in his eyes. Warmth tingled through her.

"And that...changes things?" she asked, testing the waters.

Max tossed back the rest of his drink and set the

heavy crystal on his desk with undue precision. She felt him breathe, as though he'd stolen all the air from around her for a moment, before it came back in a rush.

"Change is inevitable."

The urge to give into the pull of him, the magnetism, was overwhelming.

Before she could talk herself out of it, Emma stepped closer, raised up on her tiptoes, leveraging every inch from the platforms of her discount Louboutins.

Their breath mingled as she brushed her lips softly against his.

The sweet shock of what she'd done made her knees weak, and she steadied herself with her right palm against his chest. The hard muscle leaped beneath her fingers, like he was bracing himself for whatever came next. Emboldened by his reaction and warmed by the afterburn of the best Scotch the world had to offer, Emma leaned closer and pressed her mouth to his again, lingering this time to sample the delicious heat flickering between them.

She kept her eyes closed as she settled back into her black heels, cementing the feel of his lips beneath hers, the tingle of contact racing through her veins, even as she pulled her hand back from his chest. When she opened her eyes, he was staring down at her, controlled and handsome as ever, his face devoid of any particular expression. The way he looked at the negotiation table.

She let herself smile anyway. "I've wanted to do

that for a long time. You're right. Taking what you want is incredibly…satisfying."

He stepped even closer, and Emma's head swam from his proximity as she lifted her chin to maintain eye contact.

"Are you?" The question, delivered without emotion, caught her off guard.

"Am I what?"

"Are you satisfied? Because I'm not."

She didn't even realize that she was still holding the highball glass in her left hand until he tugged it from her numb fingers and set it on the edge of his desk. The muted thud barely registered on her consciousness as something wicked sparked in the amber gaze that held her rapt. "What's happening right now has always been…"

She didn't blink, didn't breathe, didn't move.

Time slipped by to the heavy thud of her pulse and her mind spun, desperate to fill in the blank.

Inappropriate?

Illogical?

Insane?

Max slid his hands in his pockets, the outward picture of relaxed male elegance, but when he spoke, his tone was low and rough.

"Inevitable."

CHAPTER TWO

INEVITABLE.

The word reverberated through her entire body, confirmation that Max wanted her.

She wanted him, too. All of him. All of this.

He was standing there, his eyes lit with challenge, hers for the taking. And all she had to do was reach out.

With trembling fingers, Emma grasped his tie, tugging until she'd released the silk from its Windsor knot. For the first time since this had started, she broke eye contact, dropping her gaze to the tanned column of his throat as she unfastened the first button.

Her fingers grew defter as she worked her way down the placket of his shirt, eyes hungrily following the swath of skin left in the wake of the gaping fabric—his collarbones, the smattering of dark hair across his broad chest, the ridged perfection of his abs and the intriguing trail of hair that narrowed before it disappeared behind the square buckle of his black belt.

She tugged his shirttails free from the waistband

of his pants, then dropped her hands to her sides, beholding the perfection of him. Of the moment. This was it, she realized. Her first memory. And she didn't want to forget a single detail.

Max pulled his right hand from his pocket and reached toward her. With a deftness that she found intensely erotic, he traced his finger along her skin, from her exposed collarbone down to her cleavage, the light touch singing her nerve endings.

Her whole world narrowed to the sweet friction of skin on skin and her breasts swelled against the confines of the black lace cups of her bra. She gasped at the instantaneous reaction and something wicked kindled in her belly as he began a methodical assault on her buttons, popping them open one by one until he'd reached the waistband of her skirt. He regarded his handiwork for a moment, the thin band of skin revealed by her open shirt, before unpocketing his other hand. Her breath caught in her chest as he grabbed the edges of her blouse, spreading them apart so she was exposed from neck to navel.

Max grasped her hips, then pulled her to him. The air temperature spiked from tropical to volcanic as her breasts made contact with his chest, heat rolling off him in waves. *So damn hot.* Her nipples puckered painfully against the scratchy black lace, and she sucked air into her lungs on a gasp. He smelled like sex and man and hard liquor, and the heady combination had her halfway to wherever he wanted to take her.

As if he could sense it, Max's fingers flexed against her hips before his big hands traced the side seams of her skirt. His leisurely exploration made her restless, antsy, but before she could do something about it, Max fisted the material and began the trip back up her thighs, bringing her skirt along for the ride, higher, higher, and Emma thought she might die from the slow, sweet torture of anticipation.

Cool air swirled around her legs, wringing a moan from her. *Oh God, just a little more.*

It took a second before she realized his hands had stopped moving, that he'd taken a step back. Her eyes fluttered open and she was startled by the hungry look on his face. Emma followed his gaze, realizing he'd revealed the black garter belt that held up her nude stockings.

His face was dark and his voice was rough. "You're full of surprises tonight, Ms. Mathison."

She swayed toward him as heat pooled between her legs. He always called her Emma, but this fit the fantasy that was playing out right now, and it was so perfect, so deliciously naughty, that she thought she might come.

"Yes, sir."

His head jerked up at that, eyes flaring with an emotion that Emma couldn't identify, but whatever it was, it was the first time she'd ever seen him lose that steely edge of control that was part of his legend. The jolt of it was like a lightning bolt to her core.

Whatever silly game they'd been playing was over.

In one fluid motion, he hiked her skirt up over her hips, then backed her up against his desk. The hard edge of it dug into her thighs.

Emma's teeth scored her bottom lip in anticipation, and his deep chuckle ignited something warm and twisty in her gut. "Not yet," he told her, but the promise of *soon* echoed in the timber of his voice. She sucked in a breath as his fingers traced the black elastic of her garters down to the clasp.

"These are so fucking sexy."

He was pretty fucking sexy himself, she decided as he traced the lacy edge of her stockings from front to back before his big hands gripped her thighs and boosted her onto the smooth onyx surface. It was cool against her bare skin, but her shiver had more to do with the man in front of her filling up the space between her parted knees.

She'd always known Max Whitfield was a force to be reckoned with when he had a goal within his sights, but now that she was the goal, the true depth of his focus was staggering. When he looked at her, the world narrowed to the heat in his eyes and the pounding of her pulse.

He leaned close, planting a hand on the desk on either side of her hips. Eagerness fizzed in her chest and time slowed as he wet his lips. She braced herself for impact, but it was futile. There was no preparing for Max.

He pounced like the predator she'd likened him to, devouring her mouth with such singular determination that she had to grab his shoulders to keep from falling back. Finally having her hands on him was a revelation. He was hard muscle and leashed power and it felt so damn good to touch him. To taste him.

He kissed like a man who knew what he wanted, teasing her until she welcomed the invasion of his tongue, then retreating only to start the entire process over, lowering her back onto the desk until she was almost horizontal.

Emma was so focused on his kiss that she didn't realize he'd shifted his position until his hand slipped between her legs. The brush of his thumb against the wet lace of her underwear was like the zap of a live wire, sizzling through her, and Max swore into her mouth when her hips bucked at the intimate touch.

He pulled back so quickly every part of her cried out at the loss of his touch.

She levered herself up onto her elbows.

Please. More, she wanted to say, but when she looked up at him, he was breathing hard, staring at her with such speculative intensity that she couldn't form words.

He just stood there, raking his eyes down her body. There was something so deliciously raw about being sprawled back on her elbows on his desk, her blouse spread open, her skirt pushed up around her waist, her knees spread apart and her fancy underwear on display for him.

"Don't move."

The order made her breath come faster, and she obeyed as he rounded the desk.

She spared a moment to be thankful that she'd let the saleswoman talk her into the garter belt when she'd splurged on the sexy undies, but then Max stepped back into view, his eyes full of promise and a condom packet in his hand, and suddenly she cared less about what was under her clothes and more about what was under his.

Her eyes widened as he unbuckled his belt.

Undid his pants.

Pulled himself free of his underwear.

Oh God. Yes, please.

The sight of his hand on his cock made her wet. He was so starkly beautiful, hard and masculine, and her body was vibrating for him. She pushed herself up to a sitting position as he sheathed himself with the condom, desperate to be closer to him.

His eyes cut to hers, pinning her to the spot. "I thought I told you not to move."

Emma burst into flames. She must have. Spontaneous combustion was the only explanation for the wave of heat that washed over her.

Then he grabbed her by the backs of her knees and jerked her hips to the edge of the desk, and she went molten.

Emma couldn't get enough of him. He'd been a fantasy for so long, but the reality of him surpassed everything she'd ever known. The perfect mix of heat and ice.

She wrapped her legs around his waist, slipped her hands under his shirt so she could feel the smooth expanse of his skin and let Max do what he did best: take control.

Fuck.

Things were under control until the goddamn garters. Until she called him sir. Now the woman in his arms wasn't a pleasant diversion but an all-consuming need.

Max prided himself on being disciplined, but

Emma was undoing him with nothing more than a garter belt and eyes so expressive that he could read her soul. Right now, though, it was her body that had his attention.

Her high heels digging into the backs of his legs, her hands kneading his shoulders. A scrap of black lace was all that stood between him and the kind of physical gratification that drowned out all the issues that were pounding like a nail gun in his brain—lawsuits and tech glitches and launches and the bullshit that came with righting a sinking tech company. He wanted to bury himself in her and forget the rest.

Max ran his knuckles up the inside of her thigh, stopping short of those pretty, lacy panties that had him riding the edge of anticipation.

He was so fucking turned on, galvanized by the erotic turn the evening had taken. Despite the overwhelming ache in his balls, the desperation in his muscles, he held back. Stayed perfectly, agonizingly still. Just for a minute. Just to be sure he was in control of himself. Just until she was frustrated enough that her eyes flicked from dazed pleasure to "is this happening, or what?"

Only then did he give her what they both wanted.

In one fluid movement, he slipped her underwear aside and thrust deep, his thumb riding her clit. She moaned, raking his skin with her nails, and everything faded into pure, raw sensation. The slick, scorching friction of their joining was all exactly what he needed right now. Her breath was hot on his neck.

She smelled like booze and sex, and he was ravenous for her.

Max removed his hand from between them, bracing it on the desk so he could tip her back farther. She tightened her legs around him as he sped his hips, short-stroking until she was wild beneath him. She was close. Restless and panting, clutching him to her, her lace-covered breasts scraped against his sensitized chest, driving him mad.

And Max was so goddamn ready to feel her come apart in his arms.

He shoved the fingers of his free hand into her hair, cradling her head as he laid her back, kissing her hard. He reached down, hooking his right elbow under her knee, and braced his forearm on the desk, opening her. The change in angle made her gasp, allowed him to pull out almost completely before pumping into her with slow, deep thrusts designed to push her over the edge.

"Come for me, Emma," he ordered, or maybe he begged. It didn't matter, not when he was drunk on her whiskey-flavored tongue and the pressure of her impending climax as her muscles drew tight with anticipation. *Fuck yes.* "Just like that. I want to feel you squeezing my cock."

She cried out as his words pushed her over the edge and with a groaning curse, Max gave into instinct, his chest crushing her breasts as he buried himself deep and took what he'd wanted since she'd sat on his desk, all womanly curves and dawning confidence. Pleasure exploded through his veins and he came fast and hard, his hips jerking with the aftershocks of the powerful orgasm.

It took a moment to steady his breath in the aftermath, and another moment after that before he stood, freeing her leg and helping her up to a sitting position.

She didn't look at him, and Max didn't like that it bothered him.

Frowning, he watched Emma stand, turning modestly as she adjusted things, tugged her skirt back into place, dealt with the buttons on her blouse.

Max disposed of the condom and fastened his pants but didn't bother rebuttoning his shirt or grabbing his tie from the floor beside his desk. Instead, he kept a wary eye on her body language, preparing himself for whatever awaited him when she turned around.

His decisions tonight had been deliberate—he didn't do anything without considering all the implications. But the passion that had flared between them had been...unexpected. And technically, she'd quit before anything had happened. They were both adults. The rationalization did nothing to stem his sudden unease. For the first time that evening, he wondered if he'd been right to take things as far as he had. Was she thinking the same thing?

He was expecting recriminations in those expressive blue eyes, or worse, hero worship. But when she finally turned to face him, what he saw almost dropped him to his knees. With sex-tousled hair, a misbuttoned blouse and her skirt slightly askew, Emma Mathison looked radiant and satisfied and deliciously well-fucked.

"Thanks for everything, Max." The words were husky and low, and he felt them in his groin, even before she added, "It's been a pleasure."

With her head high, her shoulders squared and a Mona Lisa smile tilting the corner of her kiss-stung lips, she walked out of his office, grabbed her purse from Sherri's desk on her way to the elevator. And she didn't look back once.

Double fuck.

Max reached for her unfinished Scotch, then downed it in one swallow.

It had been a very, very long time since he'd underestimated someone.

CHAPTER THREE

FOCUS AND DECISIVE ACTION…that was the difference between losing and winning, the difference between winning and winning big. Timing was everything. It was a lesson Max Whitfield knew better than most. He had no time for visits from the ghost-of-sexual-encounters-past.

So why the hell was he sitting there, half-hard, remembering things best forgotten?

Remembering her.

That mouth. So prim, even when it was painted scarlet.

Fuck, the things he'd wanted her to do with that mouth. Down on her knees, calling him sir with a wicked gleam in her blue eyes.

Now he couldn't look at his desk without remembering the press of the black garter belt against the pale skin of her thighs, without hearing the gasps that escaped her lips, as though she was surprised by the heat between them. He wasn't surprised. Hell, he was consumed, and he'd barely gotten his hands on her.

He exhaled at his lapse in judgment.

Taking her on his desk has been a mistake.

"Am I boring you, Whitfield?"

Max's gaze snapped to the man in the chair across from him.

Wes Brennan. Founder and CEO of Soteria Security. World-class asshole.

A brilliant asshole, obviously, but an asshole just the same.

"Not at all. I believe you were telling me about the massive breach in security you failed to prevent."

Max took an inordinate amount of pleasure at the flat, cold look that invaded Brennan's eyes.

"That spyware was caught in less than twelve hours. That's worth every zero you pay Soteria." Brennan always distanced himself from the company.

"It had goddamn better be. I want this handled."

If this got out, it would ruin him. Whitfield Industries was on the brink of reinvention. Five years after Max had ousted his corrupt father and begun to erase the era of scandal and questionable morals that had dogged the company during Charles Whitfield's reign, he was on the verge of reestablishing his grandfather's company as a leader in the world of financial services. He couldn't afford any screwups, and he certainly couldn't afford any bad press.

"Handling things is what Soteria does," Brennan assured him, like Max had insulted his honor or something.

Not that he gave a shit. The only thing Max could afford to care about right now was results.

A flash of movement in his peripheral vision tugged Max's attention to the glass door with his name on it.

"What's so important that you need me here on a Saturday afternoon?" Vivienne Grant breezed into his office, her red skirt suit almost as impeccable as her confidence.

Max allowed himself a glance at Brennan and was vindicated by the momentary crack in the man's cool facade before it was swallowed up behind bored hostility. The stiff formality that invaded the room whenever Vivienne and Brennan were present was unmistakable. He didn't know what had gone on between his chief counsel and the cybersecurity specialist, and as long as it didn't affect his business, he didn't particularly give a damn. Still, he allowed himself a moment to revel in Brennan's discomfort.

"I believe the two of you are acquainted?"

His unnecessary introduction put a hitch in Vivienne's self-assured stride, but she recovered nicely, bestowing a coolly regal nod at the other occupant of the room as she took a seat in the chair farthest from him. "Wes."

"Vivienne."

Max ignored the chill in the room. "Excellent. Now that we're all here, let's discuss our next steps."

"As I was saying, the security breach is internal. I don't think—"

Vivienne's head snapped up at Brennan's words, her eyes locking with Max's. "What *internal breach*? Do you have a suspect in mind? What the hell is going on?"

Max leaned back in his chair, forcing the relaxed pose, even though every nerve in his body was coiled tight. "We're waiting for answers."

"I might have a couple."

The voice at the door stole the attention in the room.

Jesse Hastings was Soteria Security's second in command. More personable than his business partner, Hastings was the de facto face of the company and his geniality was responsible for scoring the majority of Soteria's clients. But he really shone when you put him behind the keyboard, so when he'd insisted on helping Brennan handle this clusterfuck personally, Max had agreed. With any luck, having both of Soteria's big dogs on the case would see it resolved quickly and quietly.

"I'm just not sure you're going to like them," Hastings continued, leaning a broad shoulder against the doorjamb. "Are we waiting for Kaylee?"

The reference to his absent PR director soured his mood further. She hadn't picked up her fucking phone. If his little sister wasn't so damn good at her job, he'd have fired her when he'd purged the company of the bulk of his father's hires. "She'll be briefed first thing Monday morning. What have you got?"

"It's definitely a contained breach, but whoever's behind this is good. The information's been fragmented and rerouted through hell and back. It's going to take a while to piece together what's been leaked. But I can tell you that all the activity is localized to one computer."

Hastings raised his eyebrows, waiting until he received Max's nod to continue.

"Emma Mathison's."

Max was careful to keep his expression neutral, but his hand clenched involuntarily. Vivienne and Hastings didn't notice, but Max's jaw tightened when Brennan's eyebrow lifted with cool interest.

Smug prick.

Vivienne's face was pale when she turned back to Max. "You really think Emma sold you out? That seems…out of character. I mean, has she been acting strangely?"

Besides quitting while she lounged on his desk?

Besides her secret, self-satisfied smiles?

Besides fucking him into oblivion in thigh-highs and garters on his goddamn desk?

"She didn't sign her contract extension."

Hastings frowned at that.

"Did she say why?" Vivienne asked. "Was it something to do with her mother? She was in the hospital a while ago. Emma didn't say much about it, but she seemed worried."

His lead counsel had the kind of mind that liked to connect all the dots, but Max didn't have time for conjecture right now. He needed facts. "While I'm touched by your concern for Emma's family's well-being, let's try to stick to the salient points."

"Well, I'm not sure you're going to like those either," Jesse countered, his expression marred with concern. He walked toward them.

"I ran a couple of checks," he explained, unbuttoning his suit jacket as he took the empty seat between Vivienne and Wes. "There's a ten-thousand-dollar deposit in her primary bank account, and one Emma

Marija Mathison is booked on a plane that's leaving the country on Monday."

Max's jaw tensed. "Where?"

Jesse raked a hand through his hair, and Max could tell by the stalling maneuver that he was *not* going to like the answer.

"Croatia."

Son of a bitch. No US extradition laws in Croatia.

"Do we think she acted alone?" Vivienne was still looking for the next dot.

"The spyware is no joke," Hastings told her. "I'm going to need some time to figure out what she got and who she got it to." He glanced at Brennan. "If Wes hadn't tweaked our monitoring program, we might not have caught this at all."

Vivienne exhaled, then uncrossed and recrossed her legs. "So we've got nothing right now except that the spyware was on her computer? Any surveillance footage?"

Jesse shook his head. "Scrambled. I'll work as fast as I can to figure out what she got, but the encryption is top-notch. It's going to take more time than we have. Her flight leaves Monday morning, and we can't afford to let her leave the country, that's for damn sure."

"I can file charges," Vivienne said. "Something to stall her, but I'll need—"

Max cut her off. "No charges."

Two sets of eyes snapped toward him with surprise. Brennan remained annoyingly apathetic and glanced at his watch.

"We're two weeks out from the launch of a crypto

currency payment system that will change the way America does business." Max leaned back in his chair. "Now is not the time to ring the alarms."

Vivienne frowned, as she tucked her hair behind her left ear. She darted a glance at the security guys, though Max got the impression it was more directed at Brennan than Hastings. "A massive internal security breach happens on Emma's computer, and you're just going to let her get away with it?"

Max narrowed his eyes at the accusation, and Vivienne took a deep breath, dropping her gaze, chastened at the realization that she'd pushed him too far. Brennan's shoulders stiffened, but he was smart enough to keep his mouth shut.

Incidents involving Emma Mathison had commanded his full attention twice in as many days. And while he'd infinitely preferred last night's naked encounter over this afternoon's occurrence, letting this trend continue on any level was not acceptable.

"I want answers on Monday morning," he snapped at Brennan, waiting for the man's curt nod before skipping past Hastings, straight to Vivienne. "You're working alone on this. Wait for my instructions, and don't bring anyone else into the loop. No associates, no paralegals, no one."

"Understood."

"What about Emma? The plane ticket?" Hastings asked. "Did you want me to—"

"I want you to do your job," Max said coolly, vindicated when Hastings paled at the reprimand. Max turned his attention to the sheaf of papers on the corner of his desk. "I'll take care of Emma."

CHAPTER FOUR

MAX BANGED ON the door with more force than he'd intended.

He'd been offended by the shabby Villa Apartments that were listed as Emma's home address on her employment record. Now that he was inside the ancient building, his opinion sank even lower.

He paid her well. Better than well. There was no reason she should be living in this shithole. Which, Max realized, lent credence to Jesse Hastings's insinuations of guilt.

Despite regular paychecks from him, she obviously needed money for something, and desperation led people to do uncharacteristic things. His chest tightened at the realization that Emma Mathison wasn't finished surprising him.

Life would have been much easier if he'd kept his hands off her in the first place. He'd managed it for the last three years. Which meant fuck all, since it had taken less than five minutes after she'd resigned before he'd dragged her into his arms. It had seemed a smart play at the time.

Well, perhaps smart was overstating it, but it was low risk.

She'd quit, so she wasn't technically an employee.

This SecurePay launch had him working every waking hour. He barely had time to shower some days, let alone maintain any sort of relationship with a woman, no matter how casual. Not that what had happened between him and Emma had anything to do with a relationship. It was more like an experiment. A curiosity that needed sating.

Confirmation that their chemistry was as combustible as he'd always expected it would be. And now he was paying for that lapse in judgment.

Max heard shuffling behind the inconsequential piece of wood that was acting as a barrier between her and the outside world, but he didn't understand how something that barely blocked sound was supposed to keep her safe from intruders. Especially since the peephole was nothing more than a quarter-sized hole covered in ratty duct tape. Which was practically inviting thieves inside in this neighborhood. His left hand tightened on the sheaf of papers he held.

His musings were cut short by the slide of a chain, followed by the snick of a lock disengaging. The door swung open and there she was.

Last night's seductress was gone. In her place was a fresh-faced ingenue with impossibly wide eyes who looked like she'd stepped out of a laughably wholesome 1960s film.

His gaze slid the length of her body, from the top of her shiny blond ponytail, past her fuzzy white sweater, barely-there jean shorts and down the length of her legs until he reached the tips of her toes, painted bubble-gum pink. Max's thoughts, however, were anything but virtuous.

Every part of him that she'd touched the night before flared with heat, begging for an encore. He still wanted her. Despite everything he'd found out today. Despite the mounting evidence against her. The heat stirring in his veins iced over at the reminder, and he braced his shoulders against the onslaught of lust. He would not underestimate her again.

"Max?"

Surprised. A little breathless. But no fear. No guilt.

"What are you doing here?"

He ignored the question, shifting his focus over Emma's left shoulder at the bare, scarred walls of the old apartment. A couple of cardboard boxes were stacked in the middle of the mostly empty room. "If you needed a raise this badly, you should have told me."

Her forehead creased with puzzlement. "What? Oh." Her laugh was tinged with embarrassment. "It's a rental," she explained, moving out of his way as he stepped past her, onto the threadbare brown carpet. "I never spent much time here anyway."

Max thought back to the long hours she'd put in at the office. He'd always respected her work ethic. He gestured to the boxes. "Going somewhere?"

She nodded, closing the shoddy excuse for a door, but even as he searched her face for guile, there was none.

"On vacation, actually. Thought I'd see how the other half lives." Her smile faded at his lack of reaction, and he watched in fascination as her body language grew wary, matching his mood. She'd always been good at reading a room.

"I'm sorry. Where are my manners? Can I get you something to drink?" she asked, heading toward the outdated kitchenette.

Max foiled her attempted retreat by following her, but he stopped at the nearest side of the counter, allowing her to take cover on the far side of it. "Turns out you're going to have to reschedule that vacation. Something's come up." He tossed her contract extension on the counter between them. It landed with a heavy thud. "Sign this."

That got her attention. She stiffened, a slight frown marring her forehead as she recognized the document. "What is this?"

"Exactly what you think it is," he confirmed.

"I have a flight to Dubrovnik booked for Monday."

"Postpone it."

"I can't afford—" She stopped herself. Took a deep breath. Then restarted, the way she sometimes did in their project meetings when one of the board members wasn't taking her ideas seriously. It was the most herself Emma had been since she'd opened the door to him. Well, the most like the Emma he'd thought she was. Ever since Friday night, he wasn't sure he knew her at all.

"I am not postponing anything. I've sold almost everything I own to pay for this trip—my furniture, my clothes, my car. The lease on this place is up on Tuesday, my plane ticket is nonrefundable. I'm going to Croatia on Monday, and you have no say in the matter."

"Unfortunately, that's no longer the case. This morning, Soteria Security discovered a spyware program running on your computer."

She froze at the implicit accusation.

"It was loaded manually and discovered the day after your contract expired. The day after you formally rejected a generous extension of employment. The shallowest of security checks shows that you received an anomalous lump-sum payment of ten thousand dollars and used it to buy an open-ended plane ticket to a country with no extradition policy."

She paled with each charge, bracing her hands on the counter like she might faint. Or throw up. And despite himself, he wanted to believe in her innocence.

"Do you understand how this looks?"

"What exactly are you accusing me of?" Her voice was small, but she was heartbreakingly brave as she met his eyes.

Why he felt like he'd fallen from grace right then did not bear contemplating.

Max tipped his chin at the contract. "I'm merely offering you a way out of this. Until this security breach is resolved to my satisfaction, you will resume your role as chief analyst of research and development. We will erase everything that happened since you walked into my office and quit."

She flinched at that, and though he hadn't been referring to their hot and sweaty desk-fuck, he didn't correct her misunderstanding. It was best for everyone if they went back to their normal working relationship.

"Report to Vivienne Grant's office when you arrive on Monday morning. She can draw up an amendment to ensure you're reimbursed for the wasted plane ticket. And you can let her know if there are any further concerns we've failed to address here today. Now, sign the contract."

"Why are you doing this?"

He would not be swayed by the wounded look in her eyes. He made sure his shrug was dismissive. "It's nothing personal, Emma. It's—"

"Business?" she scoffed, her magnificent eyes glinting sharply, like daggers. "Spare me the trite maxims. Just take your bullshit contract and go."

Max took the centering breath of a sniper setting up a kill shot. "I have millions of dollars and the future of my company invested in the launch of SecurePay. The timing on this is crucial. If the media finds out we've been hacked, the project is dead in the water." Even the prospect of failure, after everything he'd sacrificed over the last five years to bring SecurePay to market, was like a hot poker to his ribs. It was enough to crack his usual icy veneer. "So until this situation has been neutralized and contained, I will do whatever it takes to ensure this launch goes off without a hitch. And that doesn't include key members of my team fleeing the country in the wake of a goddamn internal security breach!"

Her lips trembled, but she lifted her chin in a magnificent show of bravado. "I don't work for you anymore, *Mr. Whitfield.*" His name sounded toxic on her lips. "Keep your money. I don't want it. I'm leaving Monday morning, and there's nothing you can do about it."

Max respected the rally, the way her dawning anger brought a flush to her cheeks and put the spark back in her eyes.

It was too little, too late, but she didn't seem to realize that yet. He felt honor bound to make his imminent victory clear. He didn't want any misunderstandings between them.

"People who've been accused of corporate espionage usually have a hard time boarding commercial flights. Or so I've heard."

Her mouth fell open at the threat. "You wouldn't."

He kept his gaze level, implacable, until she realized the truth. That he could. And he would. It was best that she understood that from the get-go.

"You bastard."

Max accepted the epithet with a tip of his chin as he pulled a pen from his inside breast pocket and held it out to her. "Sign the contract, Emma."

She shot him a mutinous glare as she snatched the pen from his fingers, and his respect notched up again for her ability to know when she was beat. She slashed her signature across the page in black ink and shoved the contract and the pen in his direction.

Despite the heat of the movement, her eyes were ice-cold when they met his. "Get out."

Always gracious in victory, Max returned the pen to the inside pocket of his suit jacket, then picked up the papers and left.

CHAPTER FIVE

IF MAX WANTED a war, she'd give him one.

Emma's jaw was locked for battle as she strode out of Vivienne Grant's office and headed straight for the elevator. She managed a distracted smile of thanks at the man who held the door open, so she could shepherd herself and the suitcase of all her worldly possessions inside. It was born out of instinctual courtesy, not sincerity, though. Right now, smiling was the last thing she wanted to do.

Her simmering rage was evident in the jab of her thumb against the button that would take her to the top floor, where that pompous, dictatorial, gorgeous asshole she worked for was probably sitting in his swanky office, plotting new ways to infuriate her. She readjusted the straps of her leather tote against her shoulder as the silver door slid shut.

To add to her sour mood, the elevator stopped to acquire and drop off passengers on each of the four floors between Legal and her destination, dragging out the inevitable.

Emma straightened the placket of her black silk

blouse and plucked a piece of fuzz off her pencil skirt. Her sex clothes, as she'd ignominiously dubbed them.

She wasn't kidding when she'd told Max she'd purged her closet of office-appropriate attire. And that morning, when she'd been getting dressed while cursing his name, she'd liked the idea of taunting him with the outfit. It was the reason she hadn't pinned the slit in her skirt closed…or worn a bra. Small acts of rebellion designed to put him on notice. He might have forced her to come back, but he wasn't getting the mild-mannered, desperate-to-please employee she'd once been.

Now that her meeting with his bulldog of a lawyer was over, though, Emma realized the joke was on her. She might not have signed the farcical document that had been presented that morning, but she had signed the contract Max had tossed on her kitchen counter Saturday night. And Emma got the impression that Vivienne had taken an almost sadistic pleasure in laying out the terms that she'd so rashly agreed to with that hastily scrawled signature.

Emma strode out of the elevator before the door was fully open, her heels clicking against the marble tiles as she headed for her desk. Maybe one of her coworkers would loan her a damn sweater before she had to meet with—

"Emma."

Speak of the devil…

Her name sounded like a curse on Max's lips, sharp and angry, and though it jacked up her pulse, she was careful not to show it. She stopped and slid him a disdainful glance, vindicated that his deep voice sounded tight when he added, "May I see you in my office?"

It wasn't really a question, and Emma knew it, so she hesitated just long enough to annoy him. Not that she could tell if it worked. He was already back on lock-down, his handsome features an implacable mask. But it didn't matter. She was annoyed enough for the both of them.

"Of course. I'm just going to drop my purse and suitcase off at my desk, and I'll—"

"Now." Steel edged the word, brooking no opposition.

Pasting an amused smile on her lips, she shot Max's fascinated executive assistant an eyeroll. "This one's in a mood," she said, thumbing in Max's direction before stepping past him into the glass-walled office.

"See that we're not disturbed," he told Sherri, closing the door behind them.

Emma plunked herself in the closest of the visitor's chairs, bristling with coiled energy. Max, blasé as ever, took his time as he made his way to the other side of the desk. He sat, and with the push of a hidden button on the underside of the black onyx desktop, the entire expanse of glass between them and the rest of the office frosted for privacy. And then they were all alone, her itching for a fight, him cold and unaffected.

"You wanted me?"

Her double entendre landed like a gauntlet, and the scattered haze of sexual tension that was lingering in the room courtesy of their Friday night tryst coalesced into a lightning bolt of awareness arcing between them.

"What I *want*," he informed her, the bite in his voice frigid against her heated skin, "is to know what the hell you think you're doing?"

So, not completely unaffected after all.

Emma crossed her legs, enjoying the tiny victory, and the slit of her skirt parted to midthigh. Max's sightline dipped to her leg.

"Reporting for duty, *Mr. Whitfield*. As per your orders."

He raked his gaze up her body, pausing meaningfully on the peaked outline of her nipples against the black satin of her blouse, a condition made worse by his attention, before continuing up to her throat, her lips and finally meeting her eyes. Max arched an eyebrow, the gesture thick with innuendo.

"And what *duty* did you think you'd be reporting for, exactly?"

Smug prick.

Her smile was a big 'screw you' drenched in high-fructose corn syrup. "Oh, now that I'm back, I'm open to whatever *position* you had in mind. *Sir*."

The slow, feral grin that slid across his face escalated the sexual arms race they were engaged in. "Don't call me sir unless you mean it, Emma." He leaned back in his chair. "Didn't anyone ever teach you not to make promises you don't intend to keep?"

"Who says I don't intend to keep them?"

"Do you? Is that why you're wearing this delightfully indecent outfit?"

It was Emma's turn to raise an eyebrow. "It's the

same thing I had on Friday night. You didn't seem to have a problem with it then."

He ran his knuckles along his jaw. "As I recall, you were wearing a bra on Friday night. In the future, stick to the dress code."

The warning made her smile. "Here's a fun fact: there's actually no mention of undergarments in the entire policy."

She stood then, walked over to the window to give him a moment to wonder what else she may or may not be wearing, in case he had the inclination to do so. "But feel free to send me home if you feel like I'm not living up to the hallowed reputation of Whitfield Industries."

"I get the impression that you're trying to upset me."

"And why would I do that?" She tried to sound offhand as he got to his feet and joined her by the window.

"I'm not going to dissolve the contract, Emma." The words were soft. Matter-of-fact. Final. "I have too much at stake. SecurePay is going to launch next week, on time, and you are going to help me make sure it does. You signed the employment contract. If you don't want the perks you were offered this morning to go with it, that's your choice."

"Because it's insulting!" Emma whirled to face him, not in the least surprised to discover Vivienne Grant had called up to let him know how the meeting had gone, but angry nonetheless. "A residence? A driver? A clothing allowance? What your lawyer presented to me this morning was basically a mistress contract, minus the sex in return for your generosity."

His eyes narrowed dangerously at that. "I don't need to bribe women into my bed. They come when I tell them to."

The veiled reference to Friday night snapped her spine straight.

"Come for me, Emma. Just like that. I want to feel you squeezing my cock."

Bastard, she thought, even as heat uncoiled in her belly.

"You told me why you couldn't work for me. No house. No transportation. *No clothes*."

He let the last reason hang meaningfully for a moment, as though he knew her mind would conjure visions of naked skin, shifting muscles, sweaty bodies, her imaginings made all the more visceral now she knew how it felt to have Max thrusting inside her.

"I was merely trying to rectify those concerns. That's how negotiation works." He stepped closer, his nearness muddling her senses. Making her want things she shouldn't. "In order to reach an accord, sometimes one party submits to the demands of the other party."

She glared up at him, resenting the innuendo. "What happened between us wasn't a negotiation. It was a hostile takeover."

"You seemed to enjoy yourself." His voice was pure sex, and she hated him for it in that moment.

"You know what, Max? Fuck you."

"You already did," he said darkly.

And that, she realized as she turned back to the

window, was exactly the problem. He just didn't know how right he was.

If her time here was just about waiting for him to discover she wasn't the one who installed the spyware on her computer, she would have gladly stayed while Max's cybersecurity team did whatever they needed to do to prove her innocence.

The problem, however, was that the longer she stuck around waiting to be cleared for the corporate espionage she'd had nothing to do with, the more opportunity they'd have to figure out that she had, in fact, been *espionaging* in what could be construed as a *corporate-esque* manner...

When Max found out she'd been feeding carefully curated bits of information to his own father—a man he openly despised—for the entirety of her tenure at Whitfield Industries, well, it was almost enough to make a girl wish she'd been the one who'd installed the spyware on her computer.

Emma squared her shoulders, crushed the flare of guilt. She'd had her reasons for accepting Charles Whitfield's bargain, and if she had it to do over, she'd make the deal again.

Max was a big boy. With millions of dollars and an army of lawyers. He'd figure a way out of this unscathed. Her fate, on the other hand, wasn't quite so certain. She needed to take care of herself.

To that end, she injected some steel in her spine and her voice as she faced him. "You seemed to enjoy yourself," she taunted, throwing his earlier words back in his face, as though no time had elapsed since he'd spoken.

"You outrageous little—"

His hands manacled her upper arms, hauling her against him as his mouth crashed down on hers.

Emma meant to resist, truly she did, but her lips parted under the siege of angry lust, and when she raised her arms to push him away, they ended up twining around his neck and pulling him closer.

Stupid arms.

Max grabbed her ass and hauled her up his body before executing a quarter turn and shoving her back against the window. They both grunted at the rough pleasure of their bodies colliding. Emma wrapped her legs around his waist, vaguely aware that the ripping sound that accompanied the grind of his hips against hers meant the slit in her skirt was probably up to her navel now, but she was too lost in the taste and feel of Max to care.

A loud beep echoed through the room, intruding before things got really interesting, and he cursed against her mouth, letting her go so fast that she almost stumbled.

The beep sounded again, and Max stalked toward the desk, running his hands through his hair and tugging his tie straight as he reached out and hit a button on his phone, leaving Emma breathless and frustrated, and a little lust-drunk, if she were being honest. With a frown, she glanced down at her skirt.

"What?" he snapped.

The slit wasn't quite to her navel, but the frayed material made her think its fate lay with a trash can, not a seamstress. As it stood, she was going to need a couple of safety pins to finish off the workday without getting charged with indecent exposure.

Sherri's voice flooded the room. "Kaylee's here to see you. She says it's urgent. And I have Jesse Hastings on the line for your ten o'clock."

"Tell them both to wait. We're almost done here."

He hit the disconnect button and put his hands on his hips, but he didn't say anything.

"So…" Emma glanced over at the opaque glass wall. "What do you suppose Sherri thinks is happening in here right now?"

"I pay her not to speculate." And just like that, Max was all business again. "Who knows that you quit?"

Emma sighed and pushed away from the window, walking toward the front of Max's desk. By the time she'd secured her position at Whitfield Industries, the need for overtime pay and her mother's worsening condition had taken up any time she'd have used to cultivate coworkers into friends. Somehow, it had seemed easier not to bother. "If that's all you're worried about, then we're done here. I didn't tell anyone I was leaving except for you."

"Good. Let's keep it that way. If we're going to catch whoever is behind this, discretion is key."

The words snapped her like a rubber band. "What? I thought I was your suspect."

Max's amber eyes roved her face, looking for something, some answer. It felt…personal. Not like business at all.

She swallowed against the buzz of attraction that charged the air.

After what felt like an eternity, Max turned his attention to the files on his desk. "You've been cleared."

The gruff announcement blindsided her.

"What are you talking about? If you're not investigating me, why did you come to my place with that contract? Why am I here?"

When Max looked at her again, his impassive mask was back in place. "As I said, the SecurePay launch needs to go off without a hitch. And in order to unearth the mole before the release date, we need our traitor to feel confident that we are still unaware of the leak."

Hope crept through her veins. Maybe there was still a chance for her to get out of this mess with minimal damage. To Max. To herself. She just needed to keep a cool head. "So, I'm supposed to jump back into my job like nothing happened this weekend?"

She'd been expecting access restrictions, at the very least.

"Exactly like nothing happened this weekend," he confirmed.

Despite the absolution, something kept her senses on high alert, like her body was reacting to the distant clang of a warning bell that was just beyond her hearing. Something about this didn't feel right.

Emma tempered her frown at this new development and grabbed her bag from the visitor's chair. She hooked it over her forearm, positioning it strategically in front of her ruined skirt so she didn't flash anyone on the way out, pulling her suitcase with her other hand.

She was almost at the door when Max's voice stopped her.

"And Emma?"

She glanced over her shoulder, eyebrows raised in question.

"Wear a fucking bra tomorrow."

He needn't have worried. She wouldn't make that mistake again, but she kept her voice tart when she answered. "I'll wear whatever I want."

Max scrubbed a hand down his face and hit the button that summoned Sherri's voice like a high-tech genie.

"Yes, sir?"

"Tell Kaylee I don't have time to see her right now. And find out who I need to talk to about getting the dress code amended before tomorrow."

"The dress code?"

"That's what I said. Let Hastings know I'll be with him in five minutes."

Emma made sure to flash him a victorious smile as she walked out of his office, but it faded long before she reached her desk. The flare of hope she'd experienced in his office sputtered and died.

The whole point of seducing Max had been that she'd never see him again. And the whole point of quitting her job was to escape the reckoning that seemed almost inevitable now. Whitfield Industries had one of the top cyber security firms in the nation on retainer. It was only a matter of time before Max discovered what she had done.

Max dropped into the chair behind his desk, legs spread wide to accommodate the results of his earlier lack of willpower with Emma. He hit the button beneath his desk that unfrosted the wall of his office with more force than was necessary.

He was drowning in a security breach that could derail SecurePay, and here he was, acting like a horny teenager with the top suspect, about to conduct a meeting with raging erection.

"What was that all about?"

The sudden intrusion snapped his head up, and Max didn't bother to smooth the annoyance from his features as his unwanted visitor stormed in without knocking. Not that he expected such civilities from her. He might be known for his poker face, but no one taxed it quite as much as his sister.

He shot a raised eyebrow at his assistant through the glass wall, but Sherri just shrugged and turned back to her computer. Nobody stopped Kaylee when she put her mind to something. Except for their mother. Sylvia Whitfield alone held the key to deflating his impetuous little sister.

"I don't have time for this right now. I'm late for a conference call."

"Then maybe next time you have a massive security leak, you'll remember to invite your head of PR to the meeting everyone else was at. That way you won't have to make time in your busy schedule for impromptu meetings like this one."

Max settled back in his chair, accepting the inevitable.

"Jesse Hastings had some talking points delivered in case any of this gets leaked and we need to clean it up." She tossed the file in her hand onto the desk. "Why is this the first I'm hearing of it?"

"Because the first *I* heard about it was Saturday morning, and as you know, reaching my head of PR before noon on a Saturday is impossible. And since it seems that whatever it is that keeps you out until all hours on Friday nights continues to be more important than your job, I took care of things myself."

Kaylee's frown pissed him off. He wouldn't have to lecture her all the time if she'd just put some goddamn effort into doing her part to help drag Whitfield Industries into the twenty-first century.

"Just because some of us have lives," she mumbled, reminding him of her sullen younger self.

He shifted uncomfortably in his chair. Apparently teenage regression was rampant today.

"Some of us," Max countered, his voice deadly calm, "are working our asses off to make a future for this company."

Instead of a retort, Kaylee gave a heavy sigh. "Believe it or not, I didn't come here to fight with you." She dropped into one of the chairs that faced Max's desk. "So, level with me. How bad is this?"

Max raked a hand through his hair. "As bad as it gets, considering we're launching in a week. If this gets out, it will tank consumer confidence. And considering how brazen and sophisticated this one is…"

"You don't think the attack is over," Kaylee finished.

Max kept his face carefully expressionless, despite his growing ire. He had the best security firm in the business working for him, and still they were floundering for answers. But Kaylee didn't need to worry about that. He'd deal with it. "Brennan and Hastings are doing everything they can to keep you from having to use that spin degree of yours. Still, it never hurts to be prepared."

Kaylee nodded. "I agree. So don't cut me out again." She might have the power to drive him crazy, but his little sister was smart and capable. He would never have kept her on after he'd ousted their father if she couldn't hack the job. But he wasn't about to let her get the last word, either.

"Answer your phone and I won't have to. Now, get out."

Max hit the intercom button before Kaylee could argue. "Sherri, patch Hastings through."

The phone beeped a second later, and he ignored Kaylee's glare as he brought the receiver to his ear. "Hastings, Max Whitfield here. I apologize for the delay. What have you got for me?"

Max grabbed the file from his desk and held it out to her. Kaylee rolled her eyes as she snatched it from his fingers, but she got up and left.

"No problem." Hastings voice was as good-natured as ever, despite the wait. "I know this is a busy time for you. Are we good to implement?"

"Yes. I told Emma she was cleared." The lie was still bitter on Max's tongue. "Against my better judgment, so you'd better be right about this."

On the other end of the phone line, Jesse Hastings sounded much less conflicted about the situation. "Well, we're about to find out. I'm monitoring her computer remotely. I've got two camera angles on her workstation, and I can hear everything she says while she's at her desk. With any luck, she'll try to get a hold of her coconspirator, even if it's just to say that she's back in position. That should give a direction to follow at the very least."

Max thought it was a waste of time. Emma had worked for him for three years. She was a smart and methodical employee, with an incredible attention for detail. If she was the guilty party, she'd installed the spyware on her computer and walked away from Whitfield Industries with every intention of never returning, and he sincerely doubted she had any business left to attend to.

There was a reason she'd almost gotten away with it—she'd struck quickly and decisively. She certainly wasn't going to pick up where she left off when only a fool wouldn't suspect her entire workstation was bugged and monitored after what had happened. And Emma Mathison was a lot of things, but a fool was not one of them.

That being said, Max wasn't a fool, either.

And he would protect SecurePay at any cost. He'd fought for five years to bring a viable universal digital crypto currency to the market, and thanks to tireless work from his team, he was going to beat Liam Kearney's competing product to market. Whitfield Industries was poised to make the threat of credit card fraud virtually nonexistent.

Max's jaw flexed at the prospect. The cost had been steep—his father despised Max for cutting him out of the business for the blackmail scheme his dad had implemented to lock down the software on which

SecurePay was built. The extortion had ultimately led to the death of his tech mentor, John Beckett, a man Max had both liked and respected, which in turn had destroyed his friendship with John's son, Aidan, who blamed the Whitfields for the accident that had stolen John before his time.

Casualties that haunted him, even this close to the brink of success.

Max had put SecurePay above everything in his life, and if it failed…well, it couldn't. It was as simple as that.

No matter what his gut told him, he couldn't allow himself to trust Emma. Or let his body's craving for hers cloud the situation. Right now, all roads pointed to her guilt, and he would not let himself forget that she was here against her will because he'd threatened her with corporate espionage charges.

The thought made him ill. He'd spent the last five years trying to absolve himself of his father's tainted legacy, and now he was following in the bastard's footsteps. Blackmailing people to do his bidding. But there was no help for that now. He was committed to SecurePay, and he would uncover the mole in his company, no matter what it took.

CHAPTER SIX

AT PRECISELY FIVE O'CLOCK, Emma shut off her computer and gathered her things.

She'd never realized just how decadent it was, leaving work at a sane hour, though some of the mutinous joy in it was stolen by the fact that Max wasn't in his office to witness her unprecedented on-time departure.

She had to make do with Sherri's surprised, "See you tomorrow," when Emma had wished her goodnight and headed for the elevator.

The lobby was buzzing with people as she headed for the front door, her suitcase wheels bumping over the tiled floor, and she spared a moment to imagine exactly where they were going. What their lives were like. The things they'd experienced while she'd spent the last three years high in a tower, working herself to exhaustion. It had started as a way to afford the growing care requirements for her mother's worsening condition and ended as a way to distract herself from the pain of losing her mom.

And all that time, the world kept turning. People, these people, scurrying off to happy hours and dinners, rushing home to spend time with their families. Simple pleasures she'd forgotten existed.

Emma pushed through the glass door and stepped into the evening sunshine. She had no such plans. No one to meet for dinner and drinks. No one to rush home to. No home at all, she realized suddenly.

Shit.

She'd meant to look into a hotel today, but she'd been so furious after meeting with Vivienne, and then Max, and finding pins for her skirt...

A sudden prickle at the back of her neck alerted her to the presence of the tall, handsome man leaning casually against the gleaming black town car parked at the curb. He was scrolling through his phone, but as though he was privy to the same zing of awareness, he looked up, zeroing in on her before she could avert her eyes, pretend she hadn't noticed him there. Waiting. For her?

Emma hated that her skin came alive in his presence.

Max pushed away from the vehicle, tucking his smartphone in the interior breast pocket of his suit before he pulled open the door. "Get in."

She stopped in front of him. "You could try asking."

"Get in the car, Emma."

She readjusted her purse on her shoulder, so she could cross her arms.

"Please," he added tersely.

"No."

His hand tightened on the top of the door, whitening his knuckles. "Do we have a problem here?"

"You mean besides the fact that you're being a dictator…heavy on the *dick*?"

To her surprise, the churlish insult drew a flicker of a smile from him.

"You're different than you were before I had you on my desk."

His blunt musings made her frown.

"I think you mean before *I* had *you* on your desk. If you'll recall, I made the first move."

Max gave an indifferent shrug. "If you say so."

Let it go, she counselled herself. *He's just baiting you.* "I mean, I kissed you." She tried to sound nonchalant about it. "That's clearly a move. No one would classify that as *not* a move."

He tipped his head, and the arrogance of it made her bristle.

"What? What's…" Emma mimicked his action, doing her best to imbue it with the right amount of condescension.

"If that's how you want to remember it," he clarified, so supremely blasé that it sparked something in her belly.

A need to prove herself. A need to make him admit that he'd felt something shift that night, a night that had required all her courage. She needed to know that her emancipation had registered. That she'd made him want, made him burn. That she hadn't been the only one lost to the maelstrom of sensations.

She dropped her arms, stepped closer. Only a few feet of sidewalk separated them now. "That's not just how I *remember* it, that's how it happened."

"Oh really?" Max let go of the door, cut the gap

between them with a step of his own. The noise of traffic and passersby receded, replaced with the throb of her pulse, the rumble of his voice resonating in her chest.

"I *dared* you to kiss me. And despite a million reservations, you did. I like that I make you lose control."

The egotistical, patronizing, inconveniently true statement stiffened her spine. Emma's scoff was forced, born of pride and fear. "You wish."

The grin that tilted his lips was positively predatory. "Shall I prove it?"

Her body begged her to let him. Something dangerous and fizzy was working its way through her bloodstream as she swayed closer to him, desperate for a taste of the magic that seemed to spark whenever they were together. They'd unleashed something dangerous that night in his office, something Emma didn't know how to control.

Max's breathing shallowed, and his hooded gaze flicked to her mouth. He talked a good game, but he wasn't immune to what was happening between them. He might be better than her at hiding it, but the magnetism between them was not one-sided.

The blare of a horn broke the spell before their lips touched, and she jerked back from him.

He sighed. Pushed the door open wider with one hand and grabbed her suitcase with the other. "Will you get in the car now?"

Emma relented, too off-balance to do anything else. She slid into the sumptuous black leather interior, and he shut the door behind her. A muted thud behind her meant her suitcase was now being held captive in the trunk. She twisted the ring on her middle finger as she waited for Max to crawl into the back seat beside her.

The car slid away from the curb as soon as he'd pulled the door closed behind him.

"I think we need to establish some rules for our working relationship, going forward."

"Let me guess. Rule number one: wear a fucking bra?" she inquired sweetly.

The slightest frown marred his brow. "We have to keep things professional in the office. And stop being so insubordinate."

"Then stop being an asshole."

"I can see these rules are going to be difficult for you," he said drily.

"Hey, technically, I didn't break that one. We're not in the office anymore."

"You're right." Just like that, the banked fire in his eyes blazed to life, and he turned a little, angling his upper body toward her. "Come here."

The timber of his voice sent a shiver of anticipation through her.

"Don't talk to me like that." The warning was more breathless then she'd have liked.

"Like what?"

"Stay. Sit. Come. You're always ordering me around like I'm some Labrador retriever, desperate for you to pet me."

He reached up, brushed a finger along the edge of her jaw, and her breath stuttered in her lungs.

"*Are* you desperate for me to pet you?"

Oh, God, yes.

"I like it when you come, Emma."

Her heart lurched with the need to be closer, to test how near she could get before the burning consumed her.

Then her hand was on his shoulder, and his hand was on her waist, and despite the confines of the car, he was pulling her close as she levered up so that she was straddling him, her knees digging into the cushy leather seat on either side of his hips.

"I've been hard since you walked out of my office this morning," he confessed, dragging his lips against the hollow of her throat, "wondering what you've got on underneath this skirt."

Emma buried her fingers in his dark hair, hands clenching as she tried to keep her wits, tried not to drown in him. "I think you're supposed to seek medical attention when that problem persists for more than four hours."

The joke faded to a breathless rasp as he swiped his tongue against her collarbone.

"I don't need a doctor." His fingers dug into her hips. "I just need to get my hands on you so I can stop wondering exactly how many dress code infractions you're committing."

Max tried to pull her more fully against him, but her skirt held her hostage.

"I'm stuck," she whispered, looking down at the straining safety pins and gaping material along her thigh that prevented her from widening her stance.

He grabbed the hem of her skirt and ripped the slit back open, scattering the pins and freeing her.

They both groaned as she spread her knees, settling into his lap. He set his hands on her legs, tucking his fingers just beneath the edge of her skirt.

Emma's breath caught as he stared into her eyes, his palms slowly moving up her thighs, beneath her skirt, searching for answers.

Without conscious volition, their breaths had synced up, short pants of need that had her fingers clenching in his hair. She bit her lip, unable to look away from his eyes, searching hers so intensely as his hands trekked upwards, smoothing along the outside of her thighs, curving around her bare ass. He sucked in a breath, his fingers moving inexorably upward until his fingers finally encountered the lacy waistband of her thong.

"Disappointed?"

"Not even close," he assured her, tracing the band from back to front before he stroked a finger right down her center, pressing the wet lace of her panties against her core.

She gasped as sparks unfurled through her body, her hips canting forward in the search for more pressure.

He obliged her, breaching the flimsy barrier of her underwear and sliding two fingers deep inside her without further preliminaries.

She bit her lip to keep herself from crying out, because she had no idea if the glass partition between them and the front seat was soundproof, but after a few more strokes of his fingers, she stopped caring.

"You're so fucking wet," he rasped, dropping his forehead against her collarbone as he thrust inside her again and again, setting up a rhythm that had her muscles clenching in a desperate attempt to quell the need building deep inside her.

Just when she wasn't sure she could endure another second of the sharp-edged pleasure, he twisted his wrist, pressing his thumb against her clit in a circular motion that sent her spiraling over the edge.

She collapsed against him, her face tucked into the crook of his neck as she tried to catch her breath, savoring the aftershocks rippling through her body.

Finally, she found the strength to pull back, pausing just long enough to press a quick, hard kiss to his mouth before she slid off his lap and onto the seat beside him.

"Oh, man," she breathed, and he shot her a wicked grin, made even sexier because his hair was mussed, and his tie was askew. He looked disreputable. Not like the unflappable CEO of Whitfield Industries she was used to.

He leaned close, and she tilted her chin up, but he bypassed her mouth, his breath tickling the shell of her ear.

"You're going to want to pull your skirt down before Sully opens the door."

It took a moment for the import of his words to register. Along with the fact that the car was at a complete standstill. They'd arrived.

"Oh, shit."

Emma had barely gotten her skirt over her hips when the door flew open, but Max, adaptable as always, was already filling up the doorway with his broad shoulders as he got out, giving her a few precious seconds to finish restoring some semblance of order to her skirt. He stood there, blocking her from view as he exchanged pleasantries with his driver, and she used the reprieve to position her tote bag as a modesty shield before he turned and helped her out of the car.

... ...
out of the car.

CHAPTER SEVEN

EMMA'S EYES WIDENED as she joined Max on the sidewalk in front of the lavish entrance of the infamous
Berkshire Suites. She'd heard of the luxury hotel, of
course, but the reality of it was something else en-
tirely. Television footage and photographs had not
prepared her for the grandiosity of it all. "There's
more to see inside. Shall we?"

The words were a murmur, delivered softly in her
ear, sending an avalanche of shivers down her spine
and snapping her out of her open-mouthed stupor.

She turned to tell him that no, in fact, they *shan't*
do a damn thing and how dare he bring her to a hotel
to finish what they'd started in the car, a move that
was not only presumptuous, but insulting, too.

Then Max placed a hand at the small of her back,
and the possessively intimate touch hit her like the
voltage from a cattle prod. She was already up the
wide stone steps, clearing the glass doors that had
been swept out of their path by liveried doormen, and
being dazzled by her first view of the lobby before
she had the chance to say anything.

Elegant, but not subtle, the place practically oozed

money, and lots of it. It was opulence manifest—dark wood, rich brocade, intricate tilework, glittering chandeliers and vases spilling with fresh flowers. It was like something out of a movie. Who lived like this?

"Mr. Whitfield. Welcome back."

Emma shot the man beside her a sidelong glance. Well, she should have seen that one coming.

Max turned toward the distinguished, middle-aged man who strode toward them and shook his hand.

"We had the liberty of having a new key made up."

Max tucked the swipe card in his pocket.

"Thank you, Gerald. May I present Emma Mathison?"

She shouldn't like this, she told herself. The casual gallantry, the coupledom of it all.

"Welcome, Ms. Mathison," the man said with a polite nod. "If the two of you will follow me, it would be my pleasure to show you upstairs."

Everyone's eyes were on them as they headed for the elevator, and Emma double-checked that her leather tote was still covering the giant tear in her skirt.

Not that anyone was looking at her.

It was funny, she'd seen the phenomenon before, around the office. The way Max drew attention when he walked into a room. She'd always thought it was because he was the boss, but it seemed his magnetism extended into the real world, too.

Well, if you considered this playground of the rich and famous *real*, she supposed.

Max guided her into the elevator and left his hand

resting against the dip of her spine. She was starting to get used to the steady hum of connection that it caused.

"Would you prefer they take the next car, sir?" Gerald asked as two older ladies approached.

"Not necessary," Max assured him.

Gerald held the door open for the women, one tall and regal, her gray-streaked hair, one short and pleasant-looking, her white hair cut in a stylish bob.

"Mrs. Fernandez. Mrs. Tuttle. I hope you ladies enjoyed your afternoon of shopping."

"We did. Thank you, Gerald," one of the women replied as they boarded the elevator, but Emma didn't see who it was, because under the guise of making room for the new passengers, Max's fingers had trekked over to her hip and tugged her in front of him.

"Your purchases were delivered earlier," the concierge informed them as the door slid closed, "and I took the liberty of having them brought up to your rooms."

Max stepped closer. Except for the light touch of his hand, he wasn't touching her, but he might as well have been. He was like a wall of heat behind her, and her skin tingled with the knowledge that if she leaned back a scant inch or two, she'd have all that delicious muscle pressed against her from shoulder to knee.

As if he'd read her mind, his grip tightened on her waist.

The shorter lady, closest to Emma, shot her a conspiratorial wink. "If only our husbands were as attentive as Gerald here."

Emma forced herself to concentrate, to smile at the

quip, even as Max's thumb stroked a lazy back-and-forth along the top of her skirt, igniting everything that had been on simmer since they'd gotten out of the car. Since he'd given her a blinding orgasm with the same fingers that were digging into her hip.

"Also, Mr. Fernandez called to say that he and Mr. Tuttle will be later than expected, so your dinner reservation has been moved to seven o'clock."

The ladies shook their heads in unison, but they looked more amused than exasperated.

"After forty-three years of marriage, I guess that shouldn't come as a surprise," the taller woman said. "At least one of us has found a man with the good manners to be home on time for dinner. I hope this means he's taking good care of you and not leaving you alone in the city while he works all hours."

To Emma's surprise, Max's voice rumbled near her ear. "I'm definitely not leaving her alone, ma'am."

"That's excellent. Just what I hoped to hear."

Emma didn't like the way her heart bumped against her ribs at Max's kindness, indulging in small talk she would have expected him to find annoying.

She leaned back ever so slightly, giving into the heat of his body, needed the contact.

"What a lovely couple you two make."

Emma started, pulling away from Max. "Oh, we're not…"

"Thank you, ladies." Max cut in, drawing her back against him. "And I'm sure the business at hand must be very important if it's keeping your husbands away from such beautiful dinner companions."

The shorter lady tittered at the compliment. "Well,

aren't you a charming young man? Handsome, too."
She turned her attention to Emma. "This one's a
keeper," she stage-whispered as the elevator doors
slid open.

"Nice meeting you. Enjoy your dinner," Emma
managed weakly. The words came out too breathy.

"Oh, we will," the taller woman assured her as
she and her friend stepped out of the elevator. "Just
not quite as much as you will," she added, her eyes
flicking to Max as the doors slid closed behind them.

They arrived at the penthouse two floors later.

"Will you require anything else this evening, Mr.
Whitfield?" Gerald asked.

"I think we can take it from here."

"Of course, sir. Have a lovely night, Ms. Mathison."

Emma returned the nod, her knees a little shaky as
she and Max stepped out of the elevator and headed
toward the only door on the left-hand side of the hallway. They walked quickly, eagerly, and close enough
that their arms and hands brushed inadvertently along
the way, keeping her body tuned up for the main
event.

Somewhere between getting out of the car and
the elevator ride that had been a master class in fore-
play, Emma found she couldn't summon her earlier
outrage at Max's presumptuousness, because now, a
hotel seemed the perfect place to finish what they'd
started in the back seat, and she couldn't wait to get
her hands on him again.

What was happening to her?

It was like she'd opened Pandora's box to find it

contained nothing but lust and now she couldn't re-member what it was like *not* to want him.

Emma turned toward him as they arrived at the door, leaning against the wall and watching him as he retrieved the keycard from his pocket.

The lady in the elevator was wrong. Max wasn't charming—that was far too bland a description for his ability to read a room, to adapt to the situation at hand. Charismatic was a more appropriate adjective, she decided. Handsome, though, was right on the money.

The dangerous kind of handsome that grabbed her by the hormones and stoked something wild in her. She licked her lips and his eyes darkened as he stepped close. Emma lifted her chin automatically, but he bypassed her lips, and his breath ruffled the hair tucked behind her ear.

"You're leaning on the keypad." His voice was so low and sexy that it took her a second to parse the quotidian words. But before she could frown at him, he slipped his hand between her and the wall and the resulting arch of her back brought her breasts into contact with his chest. The door clicked as the lock-ing mechanism released. With a grin, he grabbed the knob with his other hand, pushing it open.

"After you," he insisted, and in retribution, she made sure to press against him as much as possible as she slipped through the doorway and into the room, reveling in his groan.

In a feat of magic, or more likely the quest for a better tip, her suitcase was already inside, looking dingy and cheap against the gleaming wooden floor.

"Wow."

It was a beautiful suite, with a top-of-the-line kitchenette to the right and a sunken living room to the left, complete with modern white-leather furniture and floor-to-ceiling windows that looked out across Los Angeles, shown off to glorious advantage in the evening light.

The snick of the door closing sounded a moment before his deep voice.

"Glad you approve."

Max stepped close behind her, stealing her attention from the killer view. Her head lolled to the side, giving his lips easy access to her neck, and he pressed a kiss there as he slid his left hand around her waist and pulled her back against his hard body.

The sensuous spell he'd woven in the elevator rushed through her with a vengeance.

Her bag slipped from her fingers, landing on the floor with a thud, and her breath came out in a rush as Max traced his finger down her right arm, from shoulder to wrist, before pressing something against her palm and curling her fingers around it.

His lips brushed her ear.

"Charge whatever you need to the room."

And then his body was gone, leaving her needy and confused and having no trouble summoning the outrage that she'd been unable to find out in the hallway.

She spun around, holding up the keycard in her hand.

"That's it?" she asked, incredulous as Max opened the door. "You're going?"

His gaze dipped to the rip in her skirt, which was now well past midthigh and working its way toward indecent. All it would take was one good tug and it would probably fall right off...

"I saw your face when we pulled up to the hotel," he said, lifting his eyes to hers. "I know why you think I brought you here, and I know how you felt about it. So yes. I'm leaving."

He stepped into the hallway.

"But if you decide you want...*anything*, my room's just on the other side of the hall."

Then he strode away, leaving the door to click shut behind him. Her body cried out at the loss.

With a frustrated sigh, she grabbed her bag off the floor and set it on the marble countertop.

Stupid body.

CHAPTER EIGHT

MAX PULLED OFF his jacket as the door to his suite closed behind him and draped the expensive fabric over the back of the couch. He needed a drink.

This thing with Emma was messing with his head. He unbuttoned his cuffs, rolling his sleeve up his right forearm, before following suit with the left.

He couldn't keep his hands off her, and when she wasn't around, he couldn't keep his mind off her. The near constant case of blue balls was distracting as hell, especially now, when he should be laser-focused on SecurePay, on bringing down whoever was trying to screw him over. And he definitely shouldn't keep ignoring the fact that it might be her.

He was just about to head for the fully stocked bar cart that sat in the far corner of the sunken living room and pour himself a glass of whatever bottle he picked up first, but a knock at his door stole his attention.

Emma.

The drink could wait.

He wet his lips. Walked to the door. Pulled it out of his way and braced a shoulder against the jamb.

"Why are you here?"

He cocked an eyebrow at her question.

"I mean, I know why you brought me here. Well, I thought I did, anyway. But why do you have a room?"

"I live here."

That surprised her. He could tell by her quick frown, the way she opened her mouth to say something, but shut it without a word, before opening it again.

"You live in a hotel?"

"I rent this floor." He shrugged. "It's close to the office."

Not that he needed to justify himself.

Emma looked down at the hallway carpet beneath her feet, then up at him. She was beautiful, and he had the urge to reach out and tuck her golden curls behind her ear, but she beat him to it.

"So, you didn't bring me to a hotel to fuck," she said, her voice soft, and the curse word on angelic lips made his cock swell.

She stepped closer. He breathed her in, and she smelled like the ocean and sun-warmed skin. Clean. Fresh. A little bit sweet.

"You brought me back to your place…"

An alluring gleam lit her blue eyes and she clasped her hands behind her back.

Max pushed the door open in wordless invitation. Lust licked at his belly as she ducked under his arm.

"…to fuck," she finished, now that she was inside.

He turned to face her.

"And that changes things?" he asked, reaching up to pull his tie off. It hit the floor with a whisper of sound, but his senses were so keyed up that it seemed louder.

She nodded, and he popped the button on his collar.

"It does, actually. You don't strike me like a man who brings a lot of women home." Emma reached for the top button of her shirt.

"And just what kind of man do I strike you as?"

"Discerning. Brilliant. Jaded." She undid another with each word. "Strong. Sexy. Good with your hands." He followed her lead until they were both out of buttons.

"But not one who gets laid often?"

He walked toward her as she tugged off her shirt, abandoning it on the floor.

No fucking bra. He didn't know what his problem was earlier, because right now it seemed an inspired sartorial choice.

Her breasts were plump and perfect, and he backed her up against the counter of the breakfast nook, not stopping until he could feel her taut nipples against his chest.

"I think you do all right for yourself."

He slid his hands up her torso before lifting her onto the marble surface.

"Just not here."

He ignored the accuracy of her assessment, let her push his shirt off his shoulders, down his arms, and when it dropped to the tile, Max's hands settled on her knees as he stepped between them, nuzzling her ear. "I've been dying to touch you."

She ran her palms over his shoulders and across his back. "All we've done lately is touch."

"Not enough. Not like I wanted to." He slid his hands up her thighs. The tear in her skirt went higher than he'd realized, and he had the sudden urge to finish what he'd started.

"Those were just appetizers," he told her, pressing a kiss to the curve of her jaw. "A quick and dirty fuck on my desk." He nipped her earlobe. "A cursory grope against the window." He dragged his tongue up her neck. "And a frantic hand job in the back of a car."

She made a sound of protest when he pulled back, but her eyes followed his movement as he grabbed either side of the frayed black material in his hands.

"I didn't get to undress you." With a sharp yank, what was left of her skirt came apart, leaving her in nothing but her teal panties.

Still too many clothes.

"I didn't get to run my hands over your body."

He skimmed his fingers across her clavicle, down the slope of her breast before palming it, giving her the pressure she craved, if her groan was anything to go by.

"And I didn't get to taste you." He kissed her shoulder as he ran his thumb back and forth over her nipple, once, twice, and she gasped at the contact.

"Do you like that?"

Her answer was no more than a whimper as he lowered his head and drew her into his mouth. Emma arched under the suction as he worked the pink bud with his tongue, and she had to grab him to keep her balance, her fingernails scoring his shoulders.

He lavished the other breast with the same attention, made her squirm under the onslaught until he had to come up for air.

"Tell me what else you want," he ordered.

Her eyes were drowsy with pleasure when they met his, and her smile was sinfully naughty. "How about I show you instead?"

She planted a hand on his chest and pushed him back a foot so she could hop down from the counter.

Emma grabbed his hand, and he followed as she tugged him across the suite, down the steps to the sunken living room, stopping in front of the floor-to-ceiling windows overlooking downtown LA. The sky was turning pink and yellow as sunset approached.

"I don't think you'll be needing these anymore," she mused playfully, unbuckling his belt and unzipping his pants. He rasped out a breath as she sent them sliding down his thighs.

Then she was on her knees in front of him, pulling off his shoes, his socks, shoving his pants out of the way before divesting him of his boxer-briefs, leaving him naked. Exposed. So goddamn ready for her.

He was *this close* to losing all semblance of self-restraint. The air vibrated with desire. Desperation. Sex.

Max's knees almost buckled at the first swipe of her tongue, and his breath escaped in a hiss as pleasure seared his every nerve ending. He reached out, bracing a hand against the window to steady himself.

He wanted to hold her there, fuck her mouth until he couldn't think anymore, just feel.

He didn't, though, because he was too close to the

edge. He didn't trust himself to control whatever she'd let loose. Not when she was making him crazy, and he couldn't get enough of her mouth.

He looked down at Emma, one hand gripping his thigh, the other at the base of his shaft, his cock disappearing between her lips. She was so fucking gorgeous.

Then, as though she could feel his gaze, she looked up at him and his hips jerked with need. It wasn't just her mouth he couldn't get enough of, it was all of her.

This woman.

If he were being honest with himself, he'd been attracted to her since the day they'd met. But it had always been in that detached way that came from knowing that it would never become anything. And once something was off the table, Max put it to the back of his mind.

But now...

"Jesus, Emma." He raked his fingers through her hair. "That's so fucking good."

She accepted the compliment by sucking him deep, driving him closer and closer to climax. His hand in her hair tightened to a fist. He didn't want to come. Not yet. Not until he was inside her.

"You have to stop."

She did, and he dropped to his knees in front of her, kissing the questioning look off her face.

"I'm not done with you yet," he assured her, before he grabbed his pants and removed the condom from his wallet.

She bit her lip as he sheathed himself, and then

he was pushing her back onto the soft, shaggy area rug beneath them, as she wound herself around him.

It felt so damn good to be in control of something where the outcome was certain, even if it was just his own orgasm. Well, his and Emma's. She was blowing his mind in all the best ways right now. Making sure she enjoyed herself was the least he could do.

Everything had been so messed up since his little coup d'état, and while ousting his father had been the right business decision, it had led to a world of trouble for Max. This security breach was the latest in a long line of annoyances, crises and calamities that he'd been wrestling under control since he'd put the old man out to pasture.

He'd been going full throttle for five years, trying to whip this project of his into reality. To prove he was right about the direction he was steering Whitfield Industries. It had been his sole focus for so long.

Until Emma Mathison had strode into his office, thrown his offer of employment in his face, and then rocked his world right off its axis.

Just like she was about to again. Because if he'd thought fucking her on his desk had been good, it was nothing compared to having her naked and writhing for him.

"Do you want me inside you?"

The words were rough on his lips, and he watched in fascination as her breath came faster. "Yes."

"Ask me for it."

"I want you to fuck me, sir."

He stared down at the amazing woman beneath him, the one who'd worked almost as many hours as he had over the last three years to make SecurePay a success, and he realized that, while it had been so perfect that night in his office, when they'd been playing their roles, all part of one night of fantasy, that wasn't what he wanted now.

"Say my name." It sounded more like a plea than an order.

"Fuck me, Max."

Oh God. That was it. He was lost. His arousal surged as he pulled her close, shoving her panties down her thighs. He needed to get so goddamn deep that neither of them could breathe.

Finally—*Jesus, finally*—he was right where he wanted to be, driving into her, stifling her moans with his mouth as he kissed her. He loved the way she wriggled beneath him, clasping him to her as she rubbed against him, letting him know that she was as turned on as he was.

This was hot, frantic. It felt so good to have Emma naked and stretched out beneath him.

When he couldn't stave off the inevitable any longer, he braced his forearm on the floor beside her head, and shoved his free hand beneath her hips, changing the angle and sending her to the stars seconds before he joined her there.

CHAPTER NINE

"I'M STARVING."

Max turned his head on the shaggy, faux-sheepskin rug, looking big and sleepy and smug. "Yeah, okay. But I need a minute."

Emma couldn't help her giggle, which was a little embarrassing, but spread out on the floor next to a man with a body that excelled at being naked, she was too sated to care. This playful side of Max was completely new to her. "I meant for food."

He grunted and slung his forearm across his eyes. "That sounds good, too."

"I'm going to order pizza." She allowed herself a moment to stare at him, all muscles and sinew, like a jungle cat in repose, before she pushed herself up off the floor and walked over to the sofa.

"Make it a large."

With a smile, she crawled onto the couch on her knees, leaning over the arm rest to grab the phone, intimately aware that Max had shifted onto his side, his head propped on his hand, his eyes roaming every inch of her skin.

"Stop looking at me like that." Her voice sounded

breathless, as though the flicker of heat in his gaze had used up the oxygen in her lungs.

"Like what?"

"Like you want to eat me."

He lifted an eyebrow in confirmation of her phrasing, and that flicker became a flame.

"I meant that you keep sizing me up." Emma did her best to smother it. "Like a panther looking for its next meal."

Max repositioned himself on the rug, his muscles shifting and bunching with the movement, doing nothing to dispel the metaphor.

"A panther?" he asked, and to her surprise, a hint of smugness laced his deep voice. "I think I like that."

She waved her hand dismissively. "Panther. Weasel. Anteater. Any kind of predator, really."

His chuckle was low, and it prickled over her skin. "Suddenly I'm less flattered."

"I'm sure your ego will recover." He was far too sure of himself for her peace of mind.

"I suspect so. My recovery time is known to be above average."

Self-preservation and non-sexual hunger had her grabbing the receiver and dialing the number she knew by heart so she could order a large Guido's Supreme with extra cheese before he managed to distract her from her task completely.

"They have pizza at the hotel," he advised as she hung up.

The look she shot him as she got to her feet dripped with reproach. "I'm sorry. This place might do a lot of things well, but there is no way they know anything about pizza."

Emma walked back toward him, caught in his gravitational pull.

"They probably make it all frou-frou, with thin-crust, and caramelized pears and goat cheese or something. I got you a real pizza. A man's pizza."

When she was close enough, he reached up and grabbed her fingers, rolling onto his back and pulling her down on top of him. He captured her mouth in a slow, deep kiss that woke her libido and sent it pacing low in her belly.

"A man's pizza, huh? You think you can handle it?"

"Please." She rolled her eyes as she slid off him so he could sit up. "I handled you, didn't I?"

Oh, Jesus. That smile.

The air left her lungs in a rush. So much for getting Max out of her system. The more she touched him, the more she wanted to touch him.

He stood up and held out a hand for her, which she accepted.

"Maybe you should handle me again," he suggested, pulling her up onto her feet and against his body in one fluid move. Then he leaned in for another decadent kiss. "How long until the pizza gets here?"

"Thirty minutes."

"Just enough time for a shower. C'mon," he said, giving her hand a tug and she realized for the first time that he hadn't let go of it during the kiss. She let him lead her out of the living room, through the hallway and the master suite, and into the bathroom, not stopping until they were standing in the most incredible shower. Sleek tiles, with a giant fixture in the ceiling above them, and several other showerheads at staggered heights.

Max reached around her to turn it on, and warm water rained over them. Emma watched, entranced, as Max tipped his face up, pushed his dark, wet hair back with both hands as water raced along the dips and planes of his body. She was caught in a beautiful storm with a beautiful man, and she didn't want to miss a moment of it.

"Got any shampoo in here?"

He tipped his chin toward a recessed space under one of the showerheads, and she noticed three nozzles.

"The left one," he instructed, and Emma reached in tentatively. It whined out a handful of delicious smelling shampoo.

"Fancy."

As she sudsed up her hair, Max shoved his palm under the nozzle on the far right and began lathering the clear gel across his chest and arms, down his stomach…lower. Body wash never looked so good, and she resented having to close her eyes to rinse her hair.

She didn't want to miss anything about this glimpse into the real Max.

He was always so elusive, and she wanted to know more about the man who ruled over Whitfield Industries. The man who pushed her, and the entire SecurePay team to do the best, be the best, every single day because he wouldn't settle for anything less.

He'd always intrigued her, but after she'd accepted Charles Whitfield's deal, after she'd realized that she'd been had, she hadn't felt she deserved to know anything personal about Max. She'd never even googled him.

But here, in this alternate universe they'd created, she gave herself permission to indulge her curiosity... just a little.

"Did you grow up around here?"

Max nodded and reached for the shampoo. His forearm slid along her upper arm, and she shivered at the contact, despite the warmth of the water.

"Beverly Hills," he provided, soaping up his hair. She should have known.

"You?"

"El Segundo." She took a chance on the middle dispenser, glad when a dollop of conditioner appeared in her hand.

"Did you like it there?"

"I have good memories, but it was hard after my dad died. The whole place kind of felt like him, you know? But my mom and I couldn't afford to leave. My parents weren't wealthy people. They worked for wealthy people." She smiled against the sad memories, working the cream rinse through her wet hair. "And now I work for you. I've been a voyeur of the life of rich people my whole life."

She'd meant it as a joke, an escape valve on a conversation too close to her heart, but the evocative nature of her comment reignited the charge in the air. A fact that wasn't lost on Max, judging by the suggestive raise of his brow.

"And? Do you like what you see?"

Hell yes.

He was wet and naked, and shampoo suds were streaming over his wide shoulders, slipping down the length of a body that had gotten her off more in the last two days than she'd managed in the two years prior.

She liked what she saw a *lot*.

Emma licked her lips and his eyes darkened. Her hands had stilled in her hair, and she had to force herself to resume finger-combing conditioner through the strands. "What's not to like?" Even to her own ears, the words sounded breathless, needy. "You fascinate me."

Max shoved his hair back from his forehead again.

"Oh?" He was surprised, and she liked that she could knock him off balance.

"You live in a hotel. You take a car service. You order your meals from room service. What sort of man sets up his entire life as a business trip?"

Max looked more contemplative than put out. "My priority is seeing that Whitfield Industries succeeds. My father did his best to kill it, and now it's my job to resurrect what's left of the business my grandfather built."

"Your job, yes. But your life?"

Now he did frown. "That's a very naive view of the situation."

"Is it? I watched my mother lose everything. She was a bright star, lovely, vivacious, full of life. And I had to stand by and watch her fade. And it didn't happen right away. It didn't happen when she wasn't fit to work anymore."

Emma held her hands under the spray of the closest showerhead, watching the drops erase the remnants of the conditioner on her palms.

"It happened when she started losing pieces of herself. She didn't remember the song we used to dance to in the kitchen while she cooked. Her eyes stopped lighting up at the mention of my father. She didn't run her fingers over the picture of him she kept beside her bed. And after a while, she looked right through me. Like a stranger."

The memory still squeezed at her heart. She'd never doubted for a second that her mother loved her, but that slow erosion had seemed far worse, far crueler, than losing her all at once.

"And it hurt. It killed me to watch her disappear, even though she was right in front of me. But I realized that, as much as it hurt to watch her lose those memories, that life she led, it was ultimately a gift. Because how awful would it be to not have any memories for Alzheimer's to steal? To not even realize that you were losing someone because nothing about them had changed?

"I want those memories, Max. I don't want my life to be an indistinguishable montage of workdays that mean nothing when I'm looking back at my life."

Max frowned. "You don't like working at Whitfield?"

Emma angled her head so that the water would rinse her hair clean. "It's been incredible. It's pushed me and challenged me. Launching SecurePay will be the culmination of work that I'm incredibly proud of. But I don't want it to be the only thing I ever did in my life. I want to walk the beaches of Dubrovnik and see where my mother grew up. I want to know that I've lived my life."

They stared at one another, water falling like rain around them, in an envelope of silence that she found surprisingly comfortable.

"I never looked at work like that. Leaving a lasting legacy has always been important to me."

She smiled at that. Leave it to this man to have such a succinct, straight-forward explanation for eighty-hour work weeks.

He stepped close, brushed his lips against hers, but when she would have kissed him back, he slid his mouth along her cheek, to her ear.

"Turn around. I think you missed a spot."

She licked water from her lips as she obeyed. God. The things this man did to her with just his voice. Made her want. Made her wet.

He kissed her shoulder as he reached for the nozzle full of body wash. Then he was running soapy palms down her back, palming the globes of her ass.

The delicious pressure over-balanced her, and she braced her hands on the slick tile in front of her.

"The pizza will be here any minute," she reminded him shakily. Reminded herself.

He slid a hand up her torso, brushing his knuckles along the underside of her breast. "I'm hungry now." His tongue on her neck made her breath catch.

"We're never going to hear the doorbell in here.

And no matter how good you are, you're never going to be better than Guido's."

"If that's a challenge, I'm up for it." He pressed his hips against her.

She did her best not to moan, flipping around to face him, the tiles chilly against the heat of her back, his body, big and warm and wet in front of her.

"Despite what you might have heard, a woman can't live on salad and sex alone."

"Who said anything about salad?" he asked, capturing her mouth and licking inside in a seductively lazy rhythm that pushed her to the brink of capitulation.

She wrapped her arms around his neck to reciprocate, but as she did, she realized the water had stopped.

"This pizza had better be life-changing," he warned, pulling back after dropping a quick kiss on the tip of her nose.

She followed his magnificent ass out of the shower, accepting the fluffy white towel he handed her. She wrapped it around her body watching as he grabbed one for himself and toweled off, gloriously, unself-consciously naked and semi-hard and in no particular hurry to cover up either fact. Not that she minded.

To be honest, she was a little sad when he finally knotted it around his hips and headed for the bedroom. She used her moment alone to wring the excess water from her hair and exchange her towel for one of the plush hotel robes on the shelf beside the shower. Then she stole his comb from the counter and restored some order to the wet tangle of her hair as she considered the pieces of Max that she'd learned, mentally fitting them into the beautiful, enigmatic puzzle of him.

The doorbell shook her out of her musing.

"Emma! Man pizza is here."

She cleaned the strands of blond hair from his comb and threw them away. It wouldn't do to leave a part of herself here. This was convenient sex and fast food. Nothing more.

"Be right out."

CHAPTER TEN

MAX GLANCED UP from the bar cart as Emma joined him in the living room. She looked fresh and lovely wrapped in the large hotel robe, her wet hair slicked back from her face. She smiled absently at him as she curled into the corner of the couch and flicked open the pizza box he'd left on the coffee table. She grabbed a slice and took a giant bite. He wasn't sure if she knew she'd verbalized her hum of pleasure as she swallowed, but every cell in his body was vibrantly aware. She was so effortlessly sensual, and it grabbed him right in the gut.

Emma chewed thoughtfully as she eyed him from her perch. She trailed her gaze from his face to his shoulders, down his bare chest, then all the way to his feet, before she swallowed.

"Never really took you for a sweatpants kind of guy," she said, drawing her legs up under her and arranging the terry cloth robe to cover them. His eyes lingered for a moment on her bare toes peeping out, before he met her gaze again. "But they're probably made of cashmere or something, huh?"

They were.

"Did you want some wine?" he offered. She nodded as she took another bite of pizza, and he poured two glasses from the bottle he'd uncorked while he was waiting for her to appear.

He joined her on the couch, placing a glass of wine on either side of the square box.

"It's so good," she encouraged, gesturing toward the pizza, her mouth full.

With a smile at her enthusiasm, he grabbed a slice. It smelled fantastic—spicy and savory—and he realized how hungry he was.

The flavor exploded on his tongue in some magic ratio of pizza toppings to grease, and he savored the glimpse of gustatory heaven. Emma hadn't been kidding. It was the best pizza he'd ever tasted.

"The greatest, right?"

"It's good," he said, downplaying the review just to enjoy the look of outrage on her pretty face. "I mean, I don't know if it's *shower-sex good*, but it's solid." He took another bite.

She rolled her eyes. "Now I know you're lying. There's no way this isn't the best thing you've ever had in your mouth."

His grin was involuntary. "You're the best thing I've ever had in my mouth, and I haven't even gotten to taste you like I want to yet."

"Stop sexualizing my pizza," she admonished with a frown, shoving the last of her pizza in her mouth.

Despite the rebuke, he noticed that she started absently spinning the ring on the middle finger of her right hand. It was a habit of hers he'd noticed lately. She tended to play with it when she was uncomfortable. Or deep in thought. He wondered which one it was right now as he finished off his slice.

"What's with the ring?" he asked, grabbing his wine glass.

Emma looked down at her right hand, back up at him. "It's my mom's wedding ring."

Not the answer he'd been expecting.

"I sold most of her stuff, but I couldn't bring myself to part with this."

"Why did you sell her things?" He took a sip of the full-bodied red.

She shrugged her shoulder, and the neck of the bathrobe parted, exposing her collarbone. "Medical bills have a way of multiplying. And they don't stop just because the treatment does." A hint of bitterness coated her grief. She looked small to him right then. Alone.

Max set his wine back on the table.

He was struck with the realization that her mother's death seemed recent enough that the emotion was still perilously close to the surface. Hadn't Vivienne mentioned something about her mother being in the hospital recently? "When?" The question fell out of his mouth without thinking, and he dreaded the answer.

She bit her lip, like she was as wary about telling him as he was about asking. But she did. "Six months ago."

Well, damn.

"Why didn't you say something?"

It was a stupid question. They'd never talked about this kind of stuff before. Personal stuff. He felt like an asshole, the vague memory of signing off on a week of vacation for her around that time worming its way into his brain. He recalled that he'd resented it. How he'd thought it was bad timing, with the Se-curePay launch approaching, and so much to do in the meantime.

"I didn't want to talk about it," she said simply.

He understood that. But he was still an asshole.

He didn't realize he'd reached for her until he felt the softness of her cheek against the back of his knuckles. He tucked her hair behind her ear.

Maybe she wanted to talk about it now.

"What was your mother like?"

The question surprised her, but in a good way, if the widening of her eyes and her lack of hesitation were any indication. "She was wonderful." She said it matter-of-factly, with no hesitation.

Max envied her certainty. It was not something he'd shared in recent memory. Of course, there must have been a time he would have answered similarly, but when he thought of his mother now, she inspired none of the warmth he heard in Emma's voice.

"You must have loved her a lot."

There was a tragic beauty to her smile. "I did. I do. My mother was an amazing baker. She used to let me help make *medenjaci* cookies. They're like Croatian gingerbread, but you make them with honey. And that smell, spicy and warm, that's what love smelled like, you know? They were my dad's favorite. He used to ask her to make them for him instead of a birthday cake, he loved them so much. And after he died, whenever I really missed him, we'd make them together."

Her smile wobbled a little, and Max's chest constricted. He very deliberately grabbed a second slice of pizza, if not quashing the temptation to comfort her, at least making it more difficult for himself.

"They met when my mother and her family came to Los Angeles on holiday, but their rental car broke down. My dad was an apprentice mechanic at the shop they got towed to. They made eyes at each other while the mechanic and her dad fiddled around with the car. They fell madly in love, and before she left a week later, he asked her to marry him."

Max paused with the pizza halfway to his mouth. "And she said yes?" He didn't mean to sound quite so incredulous.

Emma nodded. "She said yes. She was twenty, and he was twenty-two and she gave up everything she knew to stay in America. To be with him."

She stared at the ring on her finger, like she was trying to see her mother in it.

"My mom got a job as a janitor and improved her English by taking night classes. They never had very much, but they were mostly happy. As happy as people can be, I think. But even so, she always seemed a little wistful when she spoke of Croatia, about her childhood in Dubrovnik. Like she had a little bit of homesickness that never went away. I always planned to take her back there one day."

Max swallowed the pizza he'd been chewing. It was difficult to imagine a childhood more different from his own. "It's nice that you want to see where she grew up."

"What's your family like?"

He stiffened at the innocuous question. One that any person in possession of the most rudimentary social skills might ask. And the last one he wanted to answer. "Nothing like yours, I can tell you that."

The half-eaten slice in his hand was suddenly unappetizing. He set it back in the box.

"My mother is a failed politician whose career went down in a flaming scandal of newspaper headlines when she got caught fucking her handsome young intern, and my father retaliated by fucking a pretty, even-younger stripper."

A strangled-sounding "Oh" was all Emma managed at his blunt summation of the sordid story.

"Obviously, her senatorial bid came to a crashing halt before it even got off the ground. Now the only thing she cares about is propriety, and what other people think of her, and by extension, us."

Max shook his head at the ridiculousness of that particular obsession.

The damage was done. His mother of all people should realize that you couldn't rewrite the past.

If someone betrayed you, if you betrayed someone else, then the only option left was to accept the consequences and move forward as best you could.

Try as she might, and she *did* try, his mother would never escape the scandal.

Just as he would never forgive his father for what he'd done to John Beckett.

And Aidan would never forgive him.

That was how life worked.

"How old were you when it happened?"

"Ten."

He didn't deserve the heart-melting expression she was giving him, or rather, the boy he'd been. As the eldest, he'd had a lot more autonomy than Kaylee. Mostly because he thrived under rules and had always worked hard for the day when he'd be the one setting them for other people.

His sister, on the other hand, was strangled by them. And when her political career gasped out its last breath, Sylvia Whitfield had turned her considerable will to ensuring Kaylee's rebellious streak was extinguished. But try as she might to smother it, it always seemed to flare up again.

It was one of the things about his sister that Max respected the hell out of, even when it was annoying as fuck.

He used to try to help Kaylee. To intervene. Run some interference. Until his father had made it clear he would destroy anything, and anyone, Max cared about. After that, he'd learned to keep his distance.

"Kaylee was only six. And my mother's been ruining my little sister's life ever since."

And judging by the crestfallen look on Emma's face, Sylvia Whitfield had just ruined their night as well.

He took a sip of wine, but it tasted sour in his mouth. This was why he didn't talk about his family. With anyone. It was a guaranteed mood killer, especially for him.

Sex was one thing, but this… Max was a firm believer of keeping his business life and personal life separate. But whatever strange intimacy that had sprung up during their shower conversation seemed not to have dissipated completely, and just like that, he'd crossed yet another line with Emma Mathison.

A line he should have had the brains to stay far away from.

Something shifted in the room, as though he'd abolished the moment of emotional honesty with the sheer force of his will. Emma lowered her feet to the floor. The smile she shot him was reserved.

It was as though they'd both realized they'd stepped into a minefield of feelings, and retreat was their only option.

Which was probably for the best.

"It's getting late," she said.

He nodded at the lie.

"I should probably go. I've got an early morning, and thanks to my boss, I need to make sure I've got a bra to wear. He's a real stickler about the dress code."

Max forced a smile at the joke.

She got up. He did, too, though more out of a sense of propriety than a desire to hasten her departure.

"Mind if I wear this back to my room?"

His brain snapped to attention at that. "You're staying?"

"*Temporarily.* If the offer stands."

He nodded. Followed her to the door of his suite. "Stay as long as you like."

She turned to face him as she stepped into the hall. "Thanks for the pizza. I guess I'll see you tomorrow."

"Tomorrow," he repeated.

When he shut the door behind her, Max walked back to the living room to grab his wine as he contemplated the relief that washed through him when she'd said she was staying. He had a bad feeling he was in the kind of trouble you didn't know you were in until it was already too late.

CHAPTER ELEVEN

IT WAS TROUBLE all right. The full extent of which finally registered the next morning, when he found himself watching for Emma's arrival.

She'd accepted the hotel room. *Temporarily.* But according to his driver, who'd been sent back to the hotel after dropping Max at work, she hadn't accepted a ride.

Max had spent the last hour surreptitiously surveilling the elevator in between emails and phone calls. Which was how he knew it had slid open at nine sharp, to reveal Emma, looking professional as ever in her white shirt, blue pencil skirt and nude heels. She didn't glance at him as she passed, but it was done deliberately enough that he could tell she'd had to concentrate to pull it off.

The fact that it pleased him let him know he had to euthanize this ridiculous fixation immediately.

With the single-minded focus that he prided himself on, Max immersed himself in his work day. And he succeeded at keeping his mind clear of her, too. Until his four-thirty meeting with Soteria.

He set the report Brennan had just handed him on the corner of his desk as he sat.

"Give it to me straight. What are we dealing with?"

"In my professional opinion, Emma Mathison is not the originator of the hack."

Relief poured through him at the assessment.

"Not only has she got no tech or coding background that would lead me to believe she could write something this sophisticated, she also shut her computer down at eight o'clock that night. Whoever loaded the malware turned her computer back on and overrode her login. It took some time to load and her cell phone was pinging from a tower near her apartment before it should have been, considering she didn't just leave the memory stick in the computer."

No. Max could vouch for the fact that she hadn't returned to her workstation that night.

"So you don't think it's Emma, but you don't know who it is?"

"I've got Jesse digging."

"That's what you've been saying since Saturday. I don't need to tell you that it's not what I wanted to hear."

The tick in Brennan's jaw said he was well aware. "It's not what I wanted to tell you, either. Whoever did this knew what they were up against. It's sophisticated code, sure, but it was deployed in an old-fashioned way. Whoever it was had strong intel about how Whitfield Industries is set up. Us finding the leak so quickly means they lost a lot of time they would have had to siphon info. Jesse's still working on the encryption, so we should have a better idea of what they got in a day or so."

"What does this mean for the launch?"

"That's up to you. The stuff we've found so far is in the report." Brennan gestured at Max's desk. "Honestly, none of it's too damaging, information-wise, but…"

"But it's a PR nightmare if the breach hits the press," Max finished. Just what he didn't need.

Brennan shrugged. "You're going to have to decide if that's a risk you're willing to take, because from what we've uncovered so far, wrecking your brand seems to be more of the focus than stealing your tech."

Max's shoulders were rigid beneath his suit jacket. "Find out who did this. Now."

Brennan gave a curt nod and got to his feet.

Max faked a casualness he didn't feel. Soteira might not have answers yet, but perhaps a certain someone else he had working the case might be having better luck.

The second Brennan had cleared the door to his office, he pulled his secondary phone—the one that was strictly for contacting AJ—out of the hidden safe in the bottom drawer and set it on his desk.

It was a pain in the ass, but when you were working with geniuses, you put up with the quirks. And AJ definitely had her quirks. Four years ago, Soteria had caught her trying to hack into Whitfield Industries, and according to Brennan, she'd almost done it—but had gotten caught in some trap door hidden deep in the code.

He might not be Max's favorite guy on the planet, but Brennan was great at what he did, and not easily impressed. He'd helped Max track her down, and Max had set AJ up as an off-the-books consultant to help test his cyber defenses when the occasion called for it. Or, in moments like this one, to double the mind power trying to help him figure out who the hell was trying to ruin him. And he was eager to hear what his *independent consultant* had managed to unearth. He touched the screen to start a video chat.

Then, against his better judgment, he unfrosted the glass wall. Emma would be leaving soon.

It was, he realized, the first time he'd ever called AJ without having his office in privacy mode. She picked up on the first ring. AJ was always hungry for an assignment, and the more it tested her considerable skills, the better.

It was one of the reasons he let her get away with many of her other transgressions. The screen was filled mostly with her face, dark curly hair around a café-au-lait complexion, but there was enough of her T-shirt visible to prove that she was dressed in her signature all-black.

"What have you got for me?"

"I'm great, Max, thank you for asking. And you?"

He frowned at the implied condemnation and AJ got down to business.

"I don't know how she could possibly have pulled off the hack. There's nothing in her background to hint at the kind of tech genius it would take to get around anything Soteria dreamed up. I mean, not to cast aspersions, but the woman only owns a smart-phone and a tablet. You know how I feel about that."

"So she didn't code the program, but that doesn't mean she didn't install it." Max pointed out. "Any luck with the surveillance footage?"

AJ shook her head, then leaned forward so that her face took up more of the screen, obliterating any glimpse of the brick wall behind her. "I ran into the same issue Jesse had. Got nada from the security feed. Lucky for you, this is one of those times when nothing is actually something."

AJ did love a little drama. It was in such direct contrast to her life, holed up in a shitty loft that she didn't know he knew about, that it never ceased to annoy Max. He lifted an unimpressed brow. "Don't stop now. I'm on the edge of my seat."

"Oh sure, play it all casual and urbane, like you don't care. Just makes it all the sweeter when I blow your mind." AJ gave him a smug smile. "I don't think it was wiped, I think the camera was turned off. Trouble is, I can't tell if the shutdown was remote or not. But either way, we're still dealing with a manual load, which means someone was inside your building."

Max swore under his breath. Thanks to the other security precautions, Soteria didn't have anyone watching the camera feeds live. And that meant Emma was still in play as someone who had the means to have installed that spyware.

"Told you so," his hacker gloated, but her face turned suddenly serious. "What's that look, boss? Because if your gut has info that can help me out, you'd better spill."

Considering AJ had already picked up on his pre-occupation, Max led her slightly astray and gave her the other most likely suspect in the hack. "Cyber-core."

The company name was bitter on his tongue. He tended not to lead investigators down any particular path, preferring that they find it on their own. But he wanted to be sure he'd turned over every rock. Tunnel vision on Emma would do him no good. Not professionally. Or personally, he reminded himself.

"Liam Kearney, huh?" She looked contemplative for a moment. "Yeah. That fits. The douchebag is always gunning for you, and SecurePay is way ahead of his stupid payment chip. He makes spy gear, so corporate espionage seems like a weapon he'd keep in his arsenal. I'll look into him. See if anything pops. And I'm still running the security logs from that day to see if there was any unusual activity or visitors prior to the camera shutdown."

"Good. Let me know if you find anything at all."

"I will. But I still don't know why you want me to. You're paying me an awful lot of money to follow the same path that Soteria's already following. And I know that Wes Brennan's personal attention doesn't come cheap these days."

"I need to be thorough. This breach could sink Se-curePay. We're less than one week out from launch. I need this handled quickly and efficiently. You told me you're the best."

AJ lifted her chin. "Well, sure. Because I *am* the best. But double-or-nothing my fee says that Wes told you that *he's* the best."

Max nodded. "He would also point out that he's the one who caught you hacking the system."

"Hey, even a blind squirrel catches a master hacker sometimes. He got lucky. I got better."

"I'm just hoping one of you is right."

AJ frowned at him, but he ignored it. He needed results, not posturing. And he didn't want her to figure out that he'd assigned her a little side job that he hadn't brought up with Soteria. Better to let her think it was a race to the finish. AJ thrived on competition.

"Besides the grievous sin of not owning a proper computer, did anything else ring when you looked into Ms. Mathison?"

The mention of Emma had him glancing toward the elevator.

On screen, AJ shot him a look he couldn't quite decipher. "Oh, it's Ms. Mathison, is it? Okay, boss. If that's the way you wanna play it. Everything checks out in my preliminary run. Dad died years ago in a work accident, mom kicked more recently. Alzheimer's. She was staying at a really swank home that catered to that sort of thing, top of the line medical facility. Looks like your *Ms. Mathison* funneled as much of every paycheck as she could spare into the digs, including her bonus checks, hence the shithole apartment she was renting."

AJ shrugged. "After her mom died, she put together a modest funeral, and tucked half the life insurance payout away, sank the other half into a plane ticket back to her mother's homeland. Itinerary was pretty sparse. She was definitely doing her best to pull off one of those Croatia on ten dollars a day kind of trips. But I'll keep digging."

The object of his...investigation, strode past on her way out. It was precisely five o'clock. This time, instead of ignoring him, she shot him a lingering glance and a flirty finger wave as she boarded the elevator.

"Hello? Earth to Max."

His gaze snapped back to the phone.

AJ's expression was quizzical. "What was that all about?"

"Nothing." He hit the button that frosted his office glass. "Continue."

"Testy today, boss. Might wanna lay off the coffee. That stuff'll kill ya."

"AJ..." He let her name hang there, a warning.

"Fine. But I wish you'd just read the stuff I told you about before outright dismissing the idea that the government might have doctored the caffeine supply. Anyway, like I said, this is all just surface stuff. I'll follow the money and see where it leads."

"You do that. And keep it clean. I don't want Brennan and Hastings knowing that I've got you second-guessing their every move."

She scoffed. "No chance of that. I'm a goddamned ninja."

"And Brennan's a ninja slayer," he goaded, a release-valve on his frustration.

She frowned at the slight. "How many times do I have to tell you? The man knows his code, but now that he's sold out and gone corporate, he's lost his edge. Wes couldn't catch me now if he tried."

"Is that so?"

"My stealth knows no bounds," she assured him.

"In that case, I heard Aidan Beckett is back in town…" It was a long shot that this had anything to do with him, but Max let the implication dangle anyway. Better safe than sorry. As always, AJ's brilliant mind was already strategizing ten steps ahead.

"I'll tug a couple of lines, see if I can find out what brought that on."

"Get in touch if you find anything."

"I always do. So what kind of bonus do I get if I beat the esteemed Wes Brennan and find you your mole first?"

"You get me the info I need before Brennan and before this product launches on Tuesday, I'll see that the compensation matches my gratitude. And I would be very, very grateful."

AJ grinned. "That's what I like to hear. Got my eye on a new leather jacket…one that matches the interior of the new ride I'm gonna buy with your money. It's been a pleasure chatting with you, boss, but I've got to go. I've got a spy to catch."

Max sat back in his chair, contemplating AJ's information. The app was on schedule, so as long as this breach didn't hit the press, they should be good to launch next week. Still, he'd feel better if he had more answers than questions.

He shuffled some papers. Glanced through Brennan's report. Reviewed a couple of proofs the marketing department had sent over. By 5:30 p.m., he gave up and headed home.

Thanks to rush hour, it was just past six when Max arrived back at the hotel. He took the elevator to the penthouse, but instead of heading straight for his room, his gaze snagged on her door. He'd kept thoughts of her at bay for most of the day, but now he realized how close to the surface she'd been. She invaded his mind, his blood, his fantasies. Just like she'd done so often since Friday night.

Emma.

He wanted her with a disturbingly singular focus, and no matter how many times he reminded himself she might be the reason the future of SecurePay hung in the balance, it didn't lessen his desire. Because while there was a possibility she was the instigator of his problems, she was undeniably the only cure.

When she was in his arms, he could breathe. Lose himself. Forget how much was riding on Tuesday's launch and all the bullshit that accompanied it—the security breach, his father's treachery, how much he wished that John Beckett could see SecurePay come to fruition, how much he hoped that Aidan Beckett would appreciate the result of his father's work made manifest.

He approached her door, standing there like an addict, his fist raised to knock, desperate for a hit of her.

Christ, she was dangerous.

It wasn't safe to need someone this much. It couldn't be.

Max jerked his hand back from the door before he made a fool of himself. Instead, he loosened his tie and popped the button on his collar.

He didn't need her. He wanted her.

It was completely different.

And with a deep breath, he was in control of himself again. Just like he needed to be. Max pulled his wallet out as he crossed the hallway to his own room, unlocking it with his key card.

He stepped inside.

Stopped.

The air whooshed from his lungs as the door swung shut behind him.

Emma stood in the sunken living room, her body silhouetted against the window as she stared out at the Los Angeles skyline, twinkling at dusk.

Max's hands fisted. He swallowed, his throat suddenly parched.

Her hair was down, loose waves cascading over her shoulders and back. She was clad in a black bra and panties, the garter belt from Friday night holding up fishnet thigh-highs. She turned her head to the side, allowing him a glimpse of her profile as she lifted the wineglass in her left hand and took a sip.

Blood thundered in his ears when her tongue darted out to erase a drop of wine from her bottom lip. Or to fuck with him. She was too far away to tell.

When she finally turned on those black stilettos that made her legs look a mile long, his cock jerked at the sight of her—so beautiful it fucking hurt, everything about her promising sin or salvation, and in that moment, he didn't give a damn which way it shook out, as long as he got to put his hands on her.

As though in response to his thoughts, a teasing smile tilted her crimson-painted lips.

"Honey, you're home."

CHAPTER TWELVE

ONE DAY. IT HAD been one day since she'd had her hands on him, but it felt like forever. She'd done a little shopping on her lunch break, intending to grab a few more office-appropriate pieces to get her through her indentured work program. But when her thoughts turned to Max, as they so often did, there was a lot less resentment and a lot more sizzle than she'd intended.

How the hell had she managed to keep her hands off him for the last three years?

She'd snagged the fishnets from a rack near the register on a whim, and sweet-talked Gerald into letting her into Max's room by claiming he'd sent her back to grab some important paperwork that he required.

And she'd cursed herself for doing it the entire time.

The plan had been one magical night with Max. She'd only given into the attraction because it was her last day, and she had a plane ticket to the other side of an ocean.

This part—the awkward intrusion of reality—wasn't supposed to have happened.

But it had, and now things were all messed up.

She should be mad at him for the high-handed power move that had kept her trapped in Los Angeles when she should be discovering the charms of Dubrovnik.

She *was* mad at him. But she wanted him, too.

Emma wasn't sure how it had happened, when exactly he'd become a necessity. She craved him, his body, what he made her feel.

He was power incarnate, always in control, and it turned her on and drove her wild, even as it anchored her.

Then last night had happened.

The tender way he'd touched her after asking about her mother—that was some next level shit. The kind that went beyond physical gratification. And that, she could not have.

What the hell had she been thinking?

Telling him those things. Telling him about her mother. And for what? Some deluded attempt to absolve herself for the bad choices she'd made? An effort to make Max understand how hurt and lost and scared she'd been when she'd realized her mother wasn't going to get better, only worse?

To what end?

So he'd forgive her for betraying him? So he'd understand, even a little, why she'd leaked information to Charles?

He wouldn't forgive her. He wouldn't understand.

They were just fucking, she reminded herself crudely.

That's all it was, all it could be.

Telling him about her mom, wanting more, that was just a lapse brought on by a night of great sex and great pizza. It didn't mean anything. She was still in control.

And she was going to prove it right now. Prove to herself that she was in charge. Prove it to him. He could have her body. And she could have his. Nothing more.

She crossed the room, abandoning her wine on the coffee table on her way past.

"Put your hands in your pockets."

"What?"

She stopped directly in front of him.

"I said, 'Put your hands in your pockets.'"

He obeyed, and as a reward, she grabbed him by his black and grey tie, tugging him close and claiming his lips.

God, it felt good to have her mouth on him again, to breathe in his scent—the perfect combination of clean, warm man and dark, spicy cologne.

When he angled his head to take over the kiss, she pulled back.

"Uhn-uh," she chided. "In case I didn't make it clear, I'm in charge here. I'll tell you when you can kiss me. When and where you can touch. And that's strike one."

He quirked a brow at that, but he kept his mouth shut as she started walking backwards to the bedroom, pulling him along by his tie.

Max kept his eyes on hers for the entire journey, stoking the heat licking at her belly. There was something incredibly sensual about ordering a big, beautiful man around while wearing fishnet stockings.

And she was just getting started.

She tugged Max to the side of the bed before dropping his tie.

"Stay," she instructed, and his sexy mouth kicked up at the corner as he watched her take a seat on the edge of the mattress, his hands still in his pockets.

The slow, sensual beat of the song playing on her iPhone made the massive master bedroom feel more intimate. His eyes darted around the room, taking in the candles she'd placed on every flat surface, then the box of condoms on the bedside table, before landing back on her. "I take it this means I'll be playing the role of Labrador Retriever tonight?"

The reference to her admonition in the car yesterday brought an answering smile to her lips as she crossed her legs. "I wouldn't have to resort to this if you weren't so domineering all the time," she teased. "And you know what they say: turnaround is fair play."

He nodded, slow and predatory. "Why don't you turn around and get on your knees and we'll test that theory?"

The rough challenge made everything inside her clench and throb with need. "See? I haven't even gotten you out of your clothes yet, and you're already getting bossy. That's strike two. Now, take off your jacket."

He shrugged out of the immaculately tailored garment, tossing it into her outstretched hand. She closed her fingers around the soft, fine material, warm from his body, carrying with it the scent of his expensive cologne.

He reached for his tie.

"So impatient to get naked for me?"

"You don't want me to?"

Oh, she did. She set his jacket on the bed behind her, pausing as though she was considering the question.

"I'll allow it," she deigned, with her most regal nod, even as her toes curled in her stilettos as those beautiful, capable hands of his made deft work of unknotting the diagonally striped silk.

"Shirt, too," she added, as though it were an afterthought.

Watching Max strip down was a singular pleasure. He undressed like he did everything else—perfectly and precisely. No hesitation, but he didn't rush, either. He worked his way down the front of his shirt before flicking the material off his beautiful shoulders, undoing each of the buttons on his cuffs in turn, so he could pull the shirt off completely. And then he was hers to admire, muscles gleaming in the candlelight.

Lean. Powerful.

"That's enough for now."

She stood up, tugged his shirt and tie from his hand. "Take off your shoes and get on the bed."

Max toed off the gleaming black oxfords and moved the pillow out of the way before he took a seat, with his back against the headboard and his long legs stretched out in front of him.

Emma tossed his clothes on the far side of the bed as she joined him on the mattress. His eyes darkened, dropped to her cleavage while she crawled toward him until her knees were on either side of his thighs.

She leaned forward and pressed a soft kiss to his mouth.

His hands came up immediately, palms spanning the sides of her rib cage, his thumbs skating along the underwire of her bra. It took everything she had to sit back, grab his wrists, halt his lazy exploration of her body. "I told you no touching."

She pushed his hands down to the bed. "You can't help it, can you? Can't stand the loss of control. But that's strike three. And now I have to punish you."

His hands fisted against the mattress, and the bob of his Adam's apple made her want to lick his neck.

She reached for his belt, making quick work of the buckle. The slither of leather on fabric filled the room as she tugged it off him.

Her smile was wicked as she dragged the soft black leather contemplatively across her fingers.

His breathing changed—a series of shallow pants.

"I think maybe I'll tie you up," she mused, as though the idea had only just occurred to her. Emma scraped her fingernail lightly along his skin, from shoulder to biceps to forearm, then lifted his arm until his wrist was in line with his shoulder. "Teach you a lesson."

Emma licked her lips as she pressed the back of his hand against the slatted wood of the headboard, holding it there with her right hand so she could grab the belt from her lap.

His muscles drew tight as she pressed the leather

against his wrist. It took her a second to realize the jerk of his body wasn't need, it was retreat.

"Not the belt."

The harshness of his voice took her aback, and she dropped his wrist and the belt as her gaze snapped to his ashen face. There was a desperation there that scared her.

"Max?" She searched the amber depths of his eyes, trying to understand the sudden shift, but he was looking through her, breathing hard. "What's wrong?"

She cupped his cheek with her palm, angled his head up, looking for connection, trying to get him to see her. "Come back to me, baby."

He closed his eyes and his breath sawed from his lungs.

"Not the fucking belt," he repeated. But when he opened them, his eyes had lost that glassy look. Anger had replaced the fear in his voice.

She shook her head to reassure him, even as she watched him battle for control. She leaned her forehead against his. "I'm not going to hurt you," she whispered, pressing a kiss to his lips. Then another. And another. Until he kissed her back.

CHAPTER THIRTEEN

HAVING HER MOUTH on him helped. Dulled the anxiety that had jacked up his heart rate and made his palms sweat, blindsiding him with its intensity.

"You can't win big if you're soft. That's your problem. You care too much, but you can't help yourself, can you?"

He leaned into the kiss, ignored her "no touching" rule and cradled her face in his hands, shoving his tongue in her mouth with more desperation than finesse in his quest to recapture the hazy spell of lust she'd ensnared him in the moment he'd walked through the door.

"It's your fault I have to punish you. Now, stand still."

He groaned as she leaned into him, understanding his wordless plea and pressing her body against his, her arms around his neck, pulling him close as she kissed him back.

The kiss, her touch, helped calm his heart, until he could hear the music she'd put on and not just the rush of blood in his ears. The air-conditioning cooled the sweat on his skin, making him shiver.

"You'll thank me for this one day. For teaching you a lesson. For making you a man."

She was just going to tie him up. He wanted her to.

And then she'd run that fucking belt over her fingers, pressed it to his wrist and he was back there.

The bite of leather on his skin, the wash of pain along his back, biting his lip so hard to keep from crying out, from making it worse, that he tasted the salt of blood, but not tears. Never tears.

Everything jumbled together, memories and reality colliding, twisting in his gut until he couldn't tell them apart anymore.

"I'm so sorry, Max."

Emma. Emma's voice in his ear, soothing him. Emma's hands in his hair, saving him. Bringing him back.

"This was a bad idea. I never meant to… We can stop, okay? We'll stop."

Unshed tears glistened in her eyes, extinguishing all trace of the feisty seductress who'd broken into his hotel room.

No. Dammit. His father had taken too much from him already. Kaylee. John. Aidan. He wasn't taking this.

Her.

He was in control of his own goddamn life, Max reminded himself, and if he wanted to be tied up by the sexy, beautiful woman straddling his lap, then no one was going to stop him.

"Use the tie. Loose knots." His voice was hoarse.

Her fingers stilled in his hair and she shook her head.

The compassion in her eyes humbled him.

Max reached out, catching the end of his tie between his index and middle finger, pulling it free from the tangle of his shirt and lifting it between them.

"Do it."

Emma swallowed as her eyes dropped to the black and grey striped silk. Her fingers tightened against the back of his neck. She didn't want to. Probably afraid he'd freak out again.

He wouldn't.

And he needed her help to prove it to himself.

Please.

The blood rushing in his ears was too loud, so he wasn't sure if he'd spoken the word aloud, or just mouthed it.

She lowered her hands from the back of his neck, and he braced for her decision, one of the wooden slats of the headboard digging into his spine.

His breath rushed from his chest when her fingers brushed his, but he didn't look down. He couldn't break this eye contact with her, this lifeline.

She tugged the silk from his grip.

"What did I tell you about being bossy?" Her voice shook a little, but it didn't matter. All that mattered was that she was doing this for him. With him.

Emma set his hand on her thigh, palm up, and he watched as she slipped the skinny end of the tie around his wrist, knotting it so the hole was wide enough for him to pull his hand free. If he wanted to.

Her eyes met his as she pushed his wrist against the headboard again.

Her skin was warm against his.

She waited for his slight nod before she looped the tie through the wood, behind his head.

Emma lifted his other arm and repeated the process with the wide end of the tie around that wrist.

Max focused on taking deep, even breaths.

When she was done, she faced him again.

Instead of asking how he was, or worse, telling him everything was going to be fine, she just reached behind her and unclasped her bra, tossing it aside before she cupped his face and pressed her mouth to his, kissing him so deep that his brain shut off.

Desire unfurled in his belly, until there was no room for panic, not even when he wanted to touch her so badly that he strained against his bonds.

She pulled back, cheeks flushed with arousal, her kiss-swollen lips tilted in a teasing half-smile that made his blood run hot.

"No touching, remember?"

Yes. There was his flirty dominatrix. The one who'd met him in the living room and blown his mind.

"Now, let's get you out of these pants."

She reached between them and the slide of his zipper filled his ears, drowning out the music and the doubt, and he lifted his hips as she tugged his clothes down his body and all the way off.

Then she stood beside the bed and shed the layers of her pretty lingerie, until she was perfectly, gorgeously naked for him.

Crawling her way back up his body, Emma planted a knee on either side of his hips and lowered herself until the wet heat of her was pressed against his growing erection.

He groaned, the tie cutting into his wrists as she undulated her hips, rubbing against him, until she was the only thing filling his brain, until she was everything.

And still it wasn't enough. The ache inside him grew, and as if Emma could sense the slow, sweet friction wasn't enough for him anymore, her movements grew less sinuous and more desperate. He groaned, wanting everything her body was promising him.

She reached between them, and he hissed as her fingers circled his erection, her thumb swiping across the sensitive tip of him. Fire sizzled through his veins as his hips bucked, and it took him a moment to realize she's said something. Max tried to pull himself back to the surface.

"I'm on the pill," she repeated.

He couldn't breathe for a second.

"And I'm clean. And I want to feel you inside me."

His heart thudded against his ribs.

"Me, too. Christ, Emma. I need you so bad."

The exquisiteness of sliding into her with nothing between them, the tight, wet heat of her drawing him deep, the trust of it all, it wrecked him. His body was hard, but something inside him had cracked. He wanted to pull his hands free, to pound into her, to lose himself in the wildness of the act, but even as he wanted to let out the darkness, to rut, fuck, use her, let her use him, it wasn't just that anymore.

They knew too much about each other. He respected her. He liked her. And even as she was pulling him out from beneath the weight of secrets he'd kept for too long, so long that they'd changed him and warped him, he had the distinct impression he was drowning in her.

Because as much as he wanted this to be solely about sex, it was about Emma, too.

Respectful, naughty, flirty, so goddamn sweet—he'd take her any way he could get her.

He didn't deserve this. He didn't deserve to feel better.

But then she reached forward, pressing her palms to his, twining their fingers together as she rode him faster and faster, urging him on, and he couldn't stop himself from taking what she was offering—sex and forgiveness and a way to forget. At least temporarily.

"Oh fuck. Max. Please."

She contracted around him, burying her face against his neck as she cried out, and he tightened his fingers around hers as his climax rolled through him, made all the sweeter by the feel of her, so slick and tight around him as he joined her in ecstasy.

CHAPTER FOURTEEN

PREWORK SEX HAD Max feeling pretty mellow. Maybe a little too mellow, he realized, as he lost track yet again of where they were on the agenda of last-minute details that needed attending to before SecurePay went live on Tuesday.

The first time he'd done it, he'd been reminiscing about waking up with Emma in his arms, her hair tickling his chest and the curve of her ass tucked against his hips. She'd pressed his palm against her breast, and he'd kissed the back of her neck, and they'd rocked together in a slow, easy rhythm that had ended in an incredible orgasm and counted as the best wake-up call of his life.

The second offense had him reliving their back seat make-out session, which had started with her teasing him about how he'd cut himself shaving when she'd appeared wet and naked after her shower and devolved into them rounding the bases with a speed that would have impressed his fourteen-year-old self and disgusted his sixteen-year-old self. It had left Emma delightfully rumpled enough to draw a raised eyebrow from his stoic driver when he'd pulled the door open upon their arrival at work.

This latest transgression had him contemplating the merits of spreading Emma on the boardroom table after this never-ending meeting was over and shoving her skirt up her thighs, so he could finally taste her like he wanted to.

Based on the way she was glaring right now, she might not be completely amenable to the idea.

"That's ridiculous!" she burst out, as though reading his dirty mind. It took him a moment to realize the comment was directed at Jim Dawson, the head of marketing, and his earlier edict on SecurePay's ad campaign.

At least someone was paying attention to the meeting.

"Did you have something to add, Emma?" Max asked drily.

"I… I just…" She took a deep, steadying breath. Touched her mother's wedding ring. "I think that's a mistake."

Max leaned back in his chair at the head of the oval boardroom table, his gaze focused on his lone dissenter. A quick survey of the room showed that he wasn't the only one. Emma angled her chin defiantly.

He gestured for her to proceed.

"This close to launch, it's ridiculous to change the price or the marketing campaign to appeal to a wider audience. All the focus groups show that positioning this as a luxury product and a luxury price point will instill the most confidence in the buyers, even those who can't afford the product."

Jim's scoff set off some whispers around the boardroom table. "And what good are 'buyers' who can't afford your product?"

The challenge made Emma drop her eyes to the table that Max's lascivious imagination had been putting to such good use a moment ago, and for a second, he figured the matter was dropped. Then Emma raised her head, and there was a quiet poise to her that clashed with the sparks in her ocean-blue eyes.

That's my girl.

"All of my research suggests that Whitfield Industries' leadership change is going to affect this launch."

He felt the collective attention of the room on him, trying to gauge his reaction, but Max gave them nothing.

"SecurePay is not only Whitfield Industries' first salvo into the tech world, it's also our inaugural product launch with Max as CEO. It's imperative that we keep it on brand and position ourselves as a leader in the industry. When it comes to security, the data clearly shows that people are more likely to trust luxury products with luxury price tags. They associate the higher price with quality, and with the flood of copycat products that will come, it's important that we cement ourselves in the minds of the consumers as the best. Especially with Cybercore set to release their take on secure payment tech later this year."

Again, all eyes darted toward him at the mention of the rival company belonging to Liam Kearney.

Max nodded. "Agreed. We'll move forward as planned. I'll expect a report at our next meeting. And I want that glitch with the user interface taken care of. We're launching next week, and everything needs to be perfect. Thank you all for your time."

The sound of shuffling paper filled the room as people gathered their things and pushed back from the boardroom table.

"Emma. May I have a word?"

The sympathetic glances of her coworkers, save Jim, who looked rather smug, were not lost on Max as his employees filed out of the boardroom.

She just sat there, arms crossed over her perfect breasts, waiting until they were alone, and the door had swung fully shut.

"Jim is such an ass!"

"You surprised the hell out of him. Out of all of them. You've never been so vocal with your dissent before."

"Maybe I'm just done biding my time, heading back to my desk to compose carefully worded emails that stroke all of your egos while convincing you that my way is actually better," she taunted sweetly.

Her scenario struck him as familiar, as more than a few instances of her doing exactly that sprang to mind.

Huh. Funny he hadn't noticed that before.

Max nodded. "I'm glad. It's a waste of everyone's time. I much prefer having it brought up in the moment."

Emma gaped at him, searching his face for what? Some hint that he was toying with her? Max wasn't one to play games. Not out of bed, anyway.

"You're serious."

"Why wouldn't I be? I respect your opinion. I wouldn't have hired you otherwise."

She tipped her head, as if still not completely certain he was on the level. "I always got more of a 'what I say goes, so don't question it' vibe from you. Challenging you in front of your team always seemed… imprudent."

"What I say does go. But those orders are based on input from people I consider experts in their respective fields. I'm not here to be right. I'm here to win." He let a beat pass. "Besides, I like it when you get vocal."

Awareness settled in the room, warm and heavy.

"What are you doing?" she asked, though the heightened color in her cheeks told him she already knew.

He pushed his chair back from the table.

"Are you flirting with me, Mr. Whitfield?"

He rubbed his knuckles along his jaw. "The fact that you have to ask hurts my feelings a little."

Emma bit her lip to stop her smile, and his thighs flexed in response.

"I can tell. You seem pretty broken up about it."

"I'd consider letting you make it up to me."

"How generous of you," she teased, not realizing that he was dead serious.

His earlier fantasy of feasting on her right there on the boardroom table flashed through his veins, heating his blood. "It could be."

He liked the way her blue eyes darkened in response to the rough promise in his words. Despite that tell, she tried to keep her voice light. "Although

I'm intrigued by the offer, I'm afraid I'm under strict orders to keep things professional at work."

"That's a stupid rule."

She lifted a delicate shoulder. "You made it."

Max frowned at the charge. "When did I say that?"

"The other day. In the car," she added, when he continued to look blankly at her.

Oh, yeah. He had the vague recollection of saying something to that effect. "Right before I shoved my hand up your skirt," he recalled aloud.

Simpler times. Back when he still believed he had a chance in hell of outrunning this thing between them.

"Well, disregard it. It was…short-sighted of me. Especially considering that we've been flirting at work for years."

"What? No, we haven't!" She sounded shocked enough that he almost believed she believed that. *Almost.*

"Emma," he chided, getting to his feet.

"Name one time."

"You mean besides me letting you kiss me in my office?"

It was wrong to bait her, but he loved the way her eyes flashed when she was riled up. She didn't disappoint, either.

"The night you got the preliminary focus group feedback about SecurePay."

He watched the shift in her eyes as she recalled the charged moment they'd shared from across his desk when she'd given him the excellent results of her first weeks' worth of work at Whitfield Industries.

"He smiles," she'd said, almost to herself, and the air had gotten thick with...something. She'd quashed it, resurrecting her all-business facade with impressive speed, and he'd let her, because there was nothing but danger down that path. But he liked knowing she remembered it.

"That time in the elevator," he offered, circling to her side of the table.

That memory made her breath come faster. They'd been heading to the ground floor during a particularly busy afternoon, and as the elevator stopped on floor after floor, picking up more passengers, Emma had been forced to shuffle closer and closer to him as space became more prized.

Before long they'd been relegated to the back corner of the elevator, so close that the backs of their hands were pressed together, sending a jolt of awareness through him. And despite the way she kept her gaze fixed on the head of the person in front of her, he'd known she felt it, too, because even after the bulk of the passengers had exited on the sixth floor and Emma had moved away from him, she hadn't moved quite far enough to break the contact between their fingers. A forbidden touch they'd savored until they reached the lobby.

He tugged on her chair, turning her to face him. "Should I go on?"

"You remember that?" Her words were soft, and she sounded a little off balance.

He leaned forward, bracing a palm on each of the armrests, fascinated by the way the muscles in her throat worked as she swallowed.

"A man doesn't forget getting his hands on a woman like you, no matter how innocuous the touch."

She was heart-stopping when she was turned on, so pink and pretty. It was evident in the flush of her cheeks, the dance of her fingertips along her clavicle. Every cell in his body responded to the charge in the air.

Her lips parted, drawing him forward like a magnet.

"Are you wearing panties?"

"Of course," she breathed. "It's my understanding they're part of the dress code now. Sir."

The blood rushed to his cock.

"I swear to God, if I didn't have a lunch meeting in six minutes I would hike your skirt up and bend you over the table, so I could—"

Sudden movement caught his eye before he could finish his vow, and he straightened when the door to the conference room opened, ignoring Emma's perplexed look as he erected a wall of professionalism to mask the lust of a moment before.

Then the intruder showed himself, and Max lost his cool altogether.

Rage sucker-punched him in the gut, and in his peripheral vision, Emma shrank back from him, though her chair didn't move. She could probably feel the waves of animosity rolling off him. He had a weird urge to pull her behind him, to shelter her from the toxic presence that had invaded his boardroom.

He didn't, though.

Partly because she'd probably kick him for being over-protective, but mostly because he didn't want to

draw any attention to her with a snake in the room.
Instead, Max did his best to keep the bastard's attention on him by verbalizing the question that had been banging around in his brain since he'd recognized the unwelcome visitor. "What the fuck are you doing here?"

The man's oily smile made Max's jaw tighten.

"Now, is that any way to greet your father?"

CHAPTER FIFTEEN

EMMA STIFFENED.

Oh God. Not here.

She didn't need to look over her shoulder to see who was responsible for Max's deadly transformation, but she made herself do it anyway. Because like it or not, this was a nightmare she'd brought on herself.

Like his son, Charles Whitfield knew how to dominate a room. He was still in decent shape, though he'd filled out a little in the middle over the years. His salt-and-pepper hair gave him a distinguished look. She was struck, in that moment, by how similar they were physically. She'd never noticed before, because being around Charles always made her feel queasy, whereas being around Max, well…he made her feel all sorts of things.

Right now, though, all she felt was dread.

She stood, pushing the chair back into place. Emma wasn't sure what she was trying to accomplish with the show of solidarity—if she was offering Max her strength or trying to steal some of his.

Charles's gaze slid over to her, and his smugness made her feel slimy.

Max took a step forward, angling his broad shoulders like he was trying to shelter her from Charles's assessing gaze.

"And I repeat, what the fuck are you doing here?"

"I'm meeting your sister for lunch. And as far as I know, there's no reason I shouldn't be here. It's still a free country. I mean, it's not like I've been charged with a *felony* or anything." The words were a challenge, though Emma couldn't quite figure out for what.

Every muscle in Max's body looked strained.

"Now that I think of it, your sister told me to meet her in the lobby. Perhaps your lovely assistant could walk me down?"

Charles's glance sent shivers up her spine. He was toying with her, letting her know he could blow this up whenever he wanted to. His reptilian smile made her want to vomit.

"Emma is a research analyst, not my assistant," Max ground out.

Her blackmailer stepped forward, extending his hand. "I'm Charles Whitfield. Max's father. How do you do, *Emma*?"

Her stomach churned at the ludicrous pantomime. The lies clashed in her ears as she stepped forward and took Charles's hand in a farce of a handshake. He squeezed too hard, and she recognized in the flash of pain the warning he'd intended.

"She doesn't have any more time to usher you around than I do. She's on a tight deadline with a very important project and—"

"It's fine." She had to force the words out. She

didn't want to be alone with Charles Whitfield for even a second. She never did, and after what had happened between her and Max, the prospect felt a million times worse.

But she recognized in his eyes the threat of disobeying him on this...request. They were the same amber as his son's, but where Max's were fiery, Charles Whitfield's eyes were flat. Malevolent.

Max sent her a sharp glare, but she shook her head, ignoring the impulse to lay a hand on his arm. She didn't want to give Charles any more ammunition. She could already tell that he'd noticed the protective way Max had stepped in front of her.

"It's fine. Go to your meeting. I'll walk Mr. Whitfield down to the lobby."

"Come, come, Emma. No need for such formality. Please, call me Charles."

Max searched her face, but Emma nodded at the implied "are you sure?" and he relented. "Next time you and Kaylee are having lunch, meet her at the restaurant."

"Whatever you say, son. After all, you're the *boss*." Charles sneered the word, then turned and headed into the hallway.

Emma took a step to follow, but was surprised when Max grabbed her elbow, stepped close enough that she could feel his body heat along her left side. He tipped his head down, and his voice was low and steely in her ear.

"Take him straight to the lobby. No detours. I'll have security on stand-by. If Kaylee's not already down there, don't wait with him. Come straight back up. If I don't see you in ten minutes, I'm coming look-ing for you."

Then the heat of him was gone, and he'd turned his back on her, his cell phone pressed to his ear as he spoke with the head of building security.

It seemed a little excessive. Unless there was a rea-son that Max feared for her physical safety…

The realization hit hard and fast.

Emma took a bracingly deep breath to steady her-self, to keep from vomiting at the abuse Max had suffered at his father's hands. Then she stepped out into the hallway.

"Well, well, well," Charles drawled, reigniting the churning in her stomach. "My little songbird forgot to give me the most important information of all. It seems my son isn't as cold to everyone as he is to me."

"Don't call me that," she hissed, ignoring the ref-erence to whatever he might have witnessed between her and Max in the boardroom. She took off down the hallway, leaving Charles to follow in her wake. He caught up more quickly than she would have liked.

"Such a caustic reception."

"Because you make me sick!" she snapped. She'd thought he was bad enough, taking advantage of her mother's Alzheimer's, but now she could barely stand to look at him.

"Strong words. Do not delude yourself into think-ing anything has changed here, Emma. You know what's at stake."

The reminder balled her fists. Emma made herself count through the wave of fury.

"I will admit, I'm surprised to see you. Off to

chase your family history across the pond, wasn't it? Imagine my surprise when my good friend Rich Dorchester said you'd shown up, bright and early on Monday morning, just like always."

She whirled around to face him at the mention of one of Whitfield Industries' board members. "You have people spying on me?"

Charles's chuckle grated against her skin.

"Rich isn't a spy. He's a fool who can't hold his liquor, and he's happy to chat when I'm buying. When I asked him how Max was making out without you, he seemed…surprised. After that, I was suddenly *desperate* to eat lunch with my lovely daughter, just to touch base and see how she and her brother are faring. I figured I'd kill two birds, as the saying goes."

That he would mask his odious fact-gathering with parental concern made her stomach churn. Not just because she hated the idea of him running the scam on Kaylee, whom Emma liked very much, but because it was the same way he'd reeled in Emma in the first place. She'd had no reference for a parent who would put money before family. Use his daughter for information. Or take a belt to his son.

Shame swamped her as they passed Max's empty office and stepped into the elevator. She was glad to see there was a delivery guy already inside. It would keep her from having to talk to Charles. She kept her eyes forward, watching as the silver doors slid shut.

The guilt was like acid in her stomach. This was all her fault.

She was in too deep. It had seemed like nothing at the time. Leak some information to Charles. It was never anything top secret, and it was always things that were announced publicly a few days later, and for that, her mother was taken care of. Not just taken care of, she had the best care money could buy. It was a no-brainer.

The first time she'd met Charles Whitfield, she'd thought him charming. He'd seemed so sincere, telling her how worried he was about his arrogant, inexperienced son.

"Brilliant though," he'd told her, his voice gruff with pride. Or so she'd thought.

"Max wants to prove himself, but he's not as good as he thinks he is, and you've got to help him."

Charles shook his head. "I've tried, but what child wants his father to interfere? And really, I'm proud of him. It takes a lot of guts to take the reins from your old man. There's greatness in him. He's just not there yet. Still too worried what everyone thinks, and this project can't afford to have Max splitting his focus.

"He's got a lot of eyes on him, and if he fails... Well, we can't let that happen. It would destroy Whitfield Industries. For good, this time. I made mistakes, Emma. I'm not denying it. But with your help, I can avoid making the biggest one of all. A boy needs his father. Max can't see it now, but he will. And with your help, I can make sure I'm there when he comes around.

"You'll be compensated, of course. I understand your mother is unwell..."

The elevator stopped two floors down, and someone else got on.

She was a fool to have agreed. Max wasn't some

addlebrained youth, out to prove to his father who had the bigger balls. He was a force to be reckoned with, dangerously brilliant, a man who took quick, decisive action based on a thorough vetting of the information presented to him.

But thanks to an overseas trip that had kept him out of the office for the first three weeks after he'd hired her, she'd already agreed to her devil's bargain before she'd seen for herself which of the Whitfield men needed the other.

And by the time she'd realized she'd been played, she'd had to keep playing.

"Imagine if I stopped paying the other half of your mother's medical bills..."

And then, when the guilt had become too much, and she'd told him she didn't care if he sicced a horde of creditors on her, he'd changed tactics.

"It would be a shame if there was an elder abuse claim that kept you from visiting your mother."

And still, as her mother's condition had worsened, as her bad days started to outnumber the good, Emma couldn't fully regret her choices. Even with the generous salary and project bonuses that Max doled out, Emma had to live chastely to keep the debtors off her back. Without Charles's Faustian bargain, her mother would never have received the top-notch care she got at her very exclusive assisted living facility—the one that had been completely booked up until Charles Whitfield had pulled some strings.

And he'd been pulling Emma's strings ever since. Because while her mother was alive, she'd had no choice but to dance to his commands.

When her mother had finally found peace, Emma had thought she was free. But there again, Charles Whitfield had other ideas. He owned her, unless she wanted to destroy Max.

"Imagine if the press found out that my son was engaging in insider trading. I've got plenty of witnesses and a couple patsies all lined up to prove he's guilty, should it come to that."

She'd already deceived the brilliant man who'd become her boss. Ruining him was not an option.

Then her contract had expired.

Finally, the leverage had disappeared. Charles couldn't force his son to extend her contract, and she'd made damn sure that he didn't know that Max had offered her an extension. No one had known. Though it pained her, Emma had had no choice but to give up the job she loved to save the man she respected.

The man who had ignited a passion in her that she hadn't known she was capable of.

The man who had ruined her seamless escape with his high-handed orders that found her still employed.

The man she'd betrayed.

But it wasn't Max's fault. The blame lay squarely on her, though she'd tried to mitigate it as best she could. Emma had vowed to give her puppet master as little information as possible, just enough to sate him, just enough that he didn't take anything out on her mother. And she'd been keeping meticulous records of all their interactions ever since.

The elevator stopped on the eighth floor, both of the buffer occupants exited, leaving her alone with Charles.

"What the hell have you done?" Emma decided to attack first, in the hope she might be able to bully, or at least surprise him into giving up his other spy. With that knowledge, she'd have leverage again. She could help Max rid his company of traitors in one fell swoop. She'd report the perpetrator of the cyber leak, and then Emma would quit for good. And this time, nothing would stop her from boarding that plane to Dubrovnik.

Charles's voice was cutting. "You'll have to be more specific."

"You sent me here to do a job, and now you're completely undermining it! Who else do you have on the inside?"

He turned to face her, and she took an involuntary step back.

"I don't need anyone else, not now that our deal is back in effect."

"It's not. I'm done telling you anything until you tell me who else is working for you."

"That's where you're wrong, Ms. Mathison. Unless you want my son to find out what you've been doing behind his back since he hired you. And after seeing the two of you together, I suspect you don't." He narrowed his eyes at her. "Now, what is all this nonsense about me having another spy? What aren't you telling me?"

Emma shook her head, trying for nonchalance. "There was some sort of incident. Now Max has Soteria installing new security measures, which will make our deal more difficult for me," she lied, both to keep her from having to provide as much information and to figure out if Charles was part of the other leak. "I thought you might be…sourcing your information elsewhere. To someone, who unlike me, was dumb enough to get caught."

"Well, isn't that interesting? My son has enemies. Powerful ones. And if he pulls off this launch, corporate espionage will be par for the course. As I told you, he's not ready for the realities of business."

Emma squeezed her hands into fists, her fingernails cutting into her palms. How she itched to slap that smug grin from Charles Whitfield's face. Luckily, she had no doubts that Max could handle himself, and whatever was thrown at him.

"So you didn't have someone hack…his computer?" she lied at the last second. Testing him with details, but not giving him too much.

"Ms. Mathison, I'm going to teach you the secret of my success, so pay attention. You do not hack a tech company. Especially not one that has hired the likes of Jesse Hastings and Wes Brennan to protect it. Why do you think we communicate by telephone and meet in person? You don't scale guarded walls, you tunnel under them."

The elevator door slid open, and Charles sent her a questioning glance. "Aren't you going to walk me out?"

She didn't want to, but Charles made it clear that her feelings didn't have any bearing, so she stepped out of the elevator and into the lobby.

The older man's smile was venomous. "Smart choice. I'd hate to have to…*remind* you what I could do if you'd made the wrong decision."

"Dad? I told you I'd meet you in the lobby."

Emma looked up to see Kaylee Whitfield, elegant in a gray suit and pink blouse, her dark hair pulled back in a low bun, striding toward them, a slight frown marring her brow as she took in the strange twosome they made. "Hey, Emma. Do you two know each other?"

Emma forced a smile, but Charles jumped in with the easygoing charm she remembered from their first meeting. "Hello, Princess." He leaned forward, pressing a kiss to Kaylee's cheek. "I got here a bit early. Thought I'd head upstairs and say hi to your brother."

"I'm sure he was thrilled," Kaylee said drily, obviously aware of the animosity between the Whitfield men, though her joking demeanor made Emma wonder if she knew just how deep it truly went.

"He was rushing off to some meeting," Charles offered smoothly, "but Emma here offered to see me out."

Kaylee raised an eyebrow at her father. "Yes, well, you only worked here for thirty-five years. I'm sure you'd never have made it to the lobby on your own."

She shot a conspiratorial smile at Emma, even as the sudden trill of a ringtone had Kaylee pulling her purse off her shoulder. "Honestly, he's been retired for five years now, and every time we get together, all he wants to talk about is what the company's up to," Kaylee said, as she dug through her bag. "But at least he golfs sometimes. Max practically lives here and will definitely die at his desk, which has always struck me as excessive considering he doesn't even draw a salary."

Emma's eyes widened at the information.

"I'm sorry," Kaylee said holding up her cell, "but I have to take this. Thanks for helping my dad find his way out of the elevator, Em." She turned to her father as she swiped at the screen. "The driver's waiting for us. We should go," she told him, bringing the phone to her ear.

"Right behind you, Princess."

Charles turned toward Emma, pulling an envelope from the inside pocket of his suit jacket. "On second thought," he said and, under the guise of grabbing her hands in a farewell gesture, pressed the envelope into her grip, "Perhaps it's best that I remind you what's at stake here." His fingers dug into hers, and she could smell stale coffee on his breath as he leaned close and sneered. "Feel free to keep these. I have copies."

She pulled her hands from his, knuckles white.

"It was lovely to see you, Emma. As always, I look forward to working with you again."

Emma was practically vibrating as Charles sauntered off across the busy lobby. She turned her back on him, stepping into the next available elevator.

Using the couple who was riding up with her as a shield from the elevator camera, she ripped into the packet, and flipped through several photocopies of surveillance photos that Charles had obviously had taken of some of their hand-off meetings. Woodenly, Emma folded them and shoved them back inside the envelope. She might be stuck in this ruse for now, but one thing was certain: she would make that vile man pay for all his sins.

CHAPTER SIXTEEN

MAX WAS WAITING for her when she got off the elevator. Her hand gripped the manila envelope so tightly that her fingers ached, and guilt made her stiffen when he placed a hand on her lower back and escorted her into his office. Emma could feel his eyes on her, surreptitiously searching her profile. She wished she'd taken an extra minute to pull herself together after Charles's departure, to splash her face with cold water, to let some of the adrenaline of the encounter dissipate.

She dropped the offensive envelope onto the visitor chair and forced some oxygen into her lungs as Max rounded his desk to hit the privacy button. Then he was in front of her, pulling her close, and the strength of his arms, the solidity of his chest, helped soothe her jagged nerves.

"I thought you had a lunch meeting."

God, she was glad he was here.

"They'll wait. Are you okay? He didn't…you're okay, right? I shouldn't have left you alone with him."

"I'm fine," she lied, pressing closer, needing his

body heat to dissipate the chill creeping through her veins. "It was him, wasn't it?"

She knew already. But she needed to hear Max say it. She needed the rage to fortify her, so she didn't fall apart right now. "He's the one who hit you."

His muscles drew tight. His breathing was shallow. "He thought I needed to toughen up."

Emma pressed her cheek against the hard wall of his chest. "I hate him for you."

Max's hand came up to stroke her hair and she wrapped her arms around his waist, holding him until the tenseness in his body receded. Until he took a deep, even breath.

"I have to work late. Hastings wants to go over some new security precautions, and I'm booked solid this afternoon, so he's going to swing by tonight. But Sully will drive you whenever you're ready to go."

Emma leaned back, though she didn't let go of him as she lifted her head. He slid his hands up her neck to cradle her face in his palms.

"Before you call me out, that's not an order, it's a request. Tonight, I need to know you made it home safe. Okay? Can you let me have this one?"

Home.

Her throat was tight as she nodded. She hoped it was just unshed tears. "Okay."

Max pressed the softest kiss to her lips, and her eyes fluttered closed, savoring it. Letting herself pretend, just for a moment, that life wasn't so damn complicated.

He sighed when he pulled back. Her arms fell to her sides.

"I need to get to this meeting."

"Yeah. Yes. I have a lot of work to do, too." She forced a smile and made her way to the exit.

"Emma."

Her name on his lips stopped her.

She turned, and her blood iced over as Max joined her by the door, with the manila envelope in his hand.

It was all she could do not to jump back from it. Knock it to the ground. Set it on fire.

"You forgot your stuff," he said, holding it out to her.

Her fingers trembled as she accepted it.

"I'll see you later," he promised, dropping a kiss on her forehead, one final intimacy before he pulled the frosted door of his office open and they reentered the real world.

Max strode toward the elevator. Emma headed for her desk. She hugged the offensive envelope against her chest, the pressure of it over her heart her penance for all the decisions she'd made that led her here. But even through the guilt and shame, she could still feel the press of his lips against her skin.

Emma spent most of the afternoon staring blindly at her computer monitor as she tried, and failed, to make it past the first page of her summary report detailing the results of the latest SecurePay focus group.

As promised, Max's driver was outside waiting for her when she finally gave up and called it a night. On a whim, she asked him to stop at a grocery store before taking her back to the hotel.

The sadness that swamped her as she picked up

ingredients and kitchen supplies should have been her first clue that her plan to fill the time until Max got home was not her best. But her sudden need to connect to her mother was undeniable, so she persevered despite her misgivings, and between her memory and a hastily googled recipe, she gathered what she needed.

Seeing Charles today had churned up all the feelings Emma had been pushing down for so long. The way he'd exploited her mother's illness, the abuse he'd heaped on Max, her own powerlessness to go back and rectify either of those injustices, had splintered the wall inside of her—the one that let her pretend that she was okay most of the time.

Without it, all that grief, all the stress of her mother's passing was seeping up through the cracks and pooling too near the surface for Emma's peace of mind. Maybe that was part of the reason she needed this connection with her mother right now so desperately.

Her mother had always been happiest when she was baking, but it didn't take long for Emma to remember that her own fond memories of the kitchen were more about being with her mom than the act itself.

Now, surveying the wreckage of oozing honey, spilled flour and dirty dishes, misshapen cookies baking in the oven behind her, Emma felt stupid for even attempting it. For entertaining fanciful notions of domesticity while she waited for Max to come home. Like some idyllic 1950s propaganda.

Emma resented the tear trickling down her cheek.

She was such a mess, wishing for fanciful things that could never be.

This quest to make new memories was ridiculous. That wasn't how life worked. You didn't get to just wipe the slate clean and start over. You didn't get to rewrite history.

No matter how many incredible new experiences she had, it wouldn't change the fact that her mother was gone, and she would never meet Max. The lovely, vivacious Ana Petrović-Mathison she'd grown up with was already too far gone by the time she'd gotten the job at Whitfield Industries to remember Emma's stories about her handsome boss from week to week.

She couldn't just erase the fact that she'd doomed any chance of something real with Max before she'd even gotten the chance to know him. When he found out what she'd done... And the fact that she'd done it for Charles made it so much worse.

The scent of burning cookies startled her out of her dark musings, and in that moment, with smoke seeping from the oven, Emma realized that she'd failed to buy any oven mitts. By the time she'd dashed to the bathroom to grab a towel and proceeded to burn the hell out of it trying to get the cookies out of the oven without her hand meeting the same fate, her attempt at Croatian gingerbread had gone from overdone to unsalvageable.

It was only made worse by the lack of cooling racks—another item that had slipped her mind at the store—so she set the cookie sheet on the stove top with a defeated sigh, letting the bottoms of her *medenjaci* cookies finish blackening without any further attempt to rescue them. She'd just have to wait until they were cool before erasing the evidence of her failure by throwing them in the trash.

Emma wiped the tear tracks from her face and got to work. She disposed of the ruined towel before stacking the dirty bowls and measuring cups in the fancy undermount sink.

That made the kitchen look slightly less like a disaster zone, she decided. Her life, on the other hand...

What did she honestly think was going to happen here? The only reason she was still in LA was because Max was trying to save his company.

He'd blackmailed her.

She'd betrayed him.

They'd had spectacular sex.

That wasn't the start of a relationship. It was a recipe for disaster.

Distracted by her bleak thoughts, Emma grabbed the cookie sheet in her quest to clean up, yelping as it singed her skin. It fell from her hand, tumbling onto the marble floor with a loud, tinny rattle, scattering burned cookie carcasses across the gleaming tiles.

Emma sucked the tip of her stinging thumb into her mouth, so she could soothe it with her tongue while she surveyed the carnage.

Shit.

Shaking her head, she turned back to the sink to run her tender skin under the cold water.

A brusque knock on the door stole her attention a moment later.

"Emma? What's going on in there? Are you okay?"

Max.

Her heart perked up at the realization he was back.
Stupid heart.

"Emma, open up."

"I'm coming." She flipped off the tap, wiping wet fingers on her jeans as she hurried toward the sound of his voice. She fumbled with the code she had to punch into the fancy lock, but it only took her two tries before she got the door open.

He had a hand braced on either side of the jamb, and the concern on his face when he met her gaze tore a little hole in her heart. The kind that let feelings seep out.

"I heard a bang. Are you okay?"

"Yeah, that was…me," she finished lamely, thumbing vaguely behind her.

He let out a breath—relief?—and pushed back from the wall. "What are you doing?"

She moved so he could step inside. "What does it look like?"

He glanced around the disaster zone. "If I knew, I wouldn't waste either of our time asking."

Emma wilted as she closed the door. "I wanted to make the cookies my mom used to make for me. I wanted to have the memory of making cookies, damn it."

"That's very—" he took in the mess she'd made of the kitchen "—domestic of you."

She sent him a flat look and walked back to the scene of her crimes against dessert. "You could help instead of just standing there."

"I don't bake," he said, but he followed her into the kitchen.

"Not even when you were a kid?"

Max shook his head. "My mother was more of a fully catered event kind of a woman."

"Well, my mom was a great cook." She was vaguely aware she'd told him something similar the other night, but she was too busy battling the sudden helplessness trying to take control of her tear ducts to come up with anything else. "Shouldn't this be in my DNA or something? Why am I not better at this?"

He stepped forward, reaching toward her cheek.

Emma parried with a step back, bumping her hip against the counter. "What are you doing?" She didn't want to want his kindness right now. Her bruised heart couldn't stand it.

"You have flour on your cheek. Now, stand still."

His fingers were gentle against her jaw as he swiped his thumb against her cheekbone.

Emma bit her lip. Tears swam in her eyes when she finally lifted them to meet Max's gaze, but she did her best to blink them back.

"Cookie baking is harder than it looks."

"I have no doubt." He looked at her for a long time, eyes boring into hers. As though he was searching for an answer. "Okay," he said finally.

"Okay what?"

"I'll help."

Emma sucked in her breath as his big hands closed around her hips. He lifted her easily onto the counter, stepped between her legs. She would never get used to having him close. To the way her body softened when he was near.

"How is this helping?" she asked as he leaned in, his breath hot against her neck.

"I'm distracting you."

And she'd be damned if it wasn't working. She couldn't help the tiny moan that escaped as he trailed kisses up her neck.

It was erotically reminiscent of the first time Max had touched her, running his hands over her skin while she was balanced on the edge of a flat surface, her legs locked around his hips as he set her body on fire—had that really happened only a few days ago? It felt like a lifetime.

"You're getting flour on your suit," she scolded, even as she pressed her flour-marked T-shirt against his chest and wrapped her arms around his neck. He smelled delicious, clean and masculine and nothing like baking, which was everything she could've asked for just then.

"I have other suits." He slid her hips to the edge of the counter, before lifting her off it completely. "And I was going to take this one off anyway."

CHAPTER SEVENTEEN

EMMA TIGHTENED HER legs around him, and the evidence of his desire sent a spear of longing straight through her. She wanted him, like always, but tonight she needed him, too. Needed what he could give her. Needed how he made her feel.

He walked them to the bedroom, and she gloried in the strength of him beneath her hands, all shifting muscles and leashed power wrapped in a bespoke suit. She was a slave to the thrill she got from touching him, tasting him. She'd thought it was the illicitness, the taboo of bedding her boss, and maybe at the beginning it had been. Or maybe that had never been it at all. Maybe it had always been him.

Brilliant. Gorgeous. A force to be reckoned with. *Max.*

She couldn't pinpoint the moment he'd become so important to her. The first time she'd stayed late at the office without an ounce of resentment? The first time she'd earned one of his hard-won nods of approval for her work? The first inadvertent brush of his hand against hers? The first taste of his lips?

Maybe none of those. Maybe all of them.

Max stopped beside the bed, lowering her slowly until her toes touched the ground, allowing them both to savor the sinuous slide of her body against his. A pale imitation of skin on skin, but a delectable tease of what was to come.

With soft kisses and restless hands, they began tugging at each other's clothes, unfastening buttons and undoing zippers. Emma couldn't get enough. Undressing Max was like unwrapping a present. The sight of his body never failed to ratchet up her need. She couldn't help but lean forward and press a kiss to his pec, just above his heart, even as he sent her jeans sliding down her hips.

When they were finally naked, Max pulled her close, walking her backward until the mattress brushed the backs of her thighs. Unlike their previous sexual encounters, there was a gravitas to this one that Emma couldn't deny. There was still the pure, unadulterated want that she was used to whenever she touched him, but this was deeper, somehow, less frenzied. As though their passion had matured into something more potent.

He followed her onto the bed, and he was so beautiful, all hard planes and sinewy muscles, his jungle cat grace in evidence again as he moved over her. Their legs tangled together as he ran a hand along her skin, from her hip, up her side until he palmed her breast.

And suddenly, time slowed down.

Tonight, there were none of the dirty words, no words at all, just the soundtrack of their mingled breaths, of her heart beating steady and true.

Sweet kisses and lingering caresses. A slow worship of each other's bodies.

She twined her fingers in his hair as his mouth paid homage to her breast. Each flick of his tongue against her nipple launching a spear of pleasure straight to her core. She shuddered as he traced her areola with the tip of his tongue, then kissed his way to her other breast to accord it the same decadent treatment.

For the first time in a long time, she felt like herself again. Like a woman who could handle things. The realization surprised her, since not ten minutes ago she'd been on the verge of sobbing, cookies spilled across the floor, failing so spectacularly at her task that she'd been ready to give up.

She wanted to devour him, but when she tried to pull him up so she could get her mouth on his, he shook his head.

"Not yet," he told her, in response to her mewl of frustration when he stayed put. "There's something I've been meaning to do, and I'm not going to let you distract me with that pretty mouth of yours until I'm finished."

He slid a little farther down her body, pressing a promissory kiss just above her belly button, and another beneath it. Emma's muscles tensed with anticipation, her fingers curling preemptively against the mattress.

Max settled himself between her legs, and she had to bend her knees to accommodate the breadth of his shoulders. The low throb of greed drummed at the apex of her thighs. She wanted everything he was poised to give her, and she shifted restlessly beneath him, wishing he'd just get on with it already. Not until she felt his breath against the wet heat of her did she realize that she'd closed her eyes. With conscious effort, she forced them open, and the second she did, he lowered his head and licked straight up the center of her.

Stars exploded through her body and she raked her fingernails against the bedspread as her back arched with the sharpness of her need.

Her muscles grew drowsy with pleasure as he shifted his technique, teasing her with only the tip of his tongue, dragging her to the brink before retreating, only to start the process over again. Driving her wild with the electric touch of his mouth and the delicious scrape of his five o'clock shadow against her inner thighs.

The orgasm building inside her was different from the ones before. This one rolled along her nerve endings, slow but powerful, and just out of reach.

She reached for him, burying her fingers in his wavy black hair, with half a mind to push him away because she wasn't sure she could endure another second on the edge of this precipice, and half a mind to hold him right where he was forever and ever.

Before she could decide, his tongue was replaced with the gentle suction of his lips against her clit as his finger sank deep inside her, and the dual sensation of soft and hard, push and pull, sent her climax rushing through her like waves breaking across her skin, and she gasped as she let herself drown in the sweet perfection of it.

He crawled back up her body, lying on his side

next to her. She rolled to face him, and the intensity in his amber gaze made her feel like he'd branded her, claimed her. Made her doubt that anyone else in the world could make her feel like he had.

Emma trembled at the thought.

"I've been dreaming about that since we met." He reached over and pushed a strand of hair off her cheek.

Max Whitfield. Slayer of words. "Liar." Her heart flipped happily as she made the accusation.

"Well, I've been dreaming about it *more* since we met naked."

"I'm happy to make your dream a reality anytime," she teased, pushing up onto her elbow.

She leaned close and breathed in his warmth, nuzzling his jaw, pressing her lips to the pulse at the base of his neck.

It was heaven to have her mouth on his skin, to be able to touch him when she wanted. How she wanted.

Emma caught his bottom lip between her teeth, then kissed him slow, deep, wet. He groaned as he shifted onto his back, and she liked knowing he was as desperate as she was for the culmination of the lust that overtook her whenever he was within arm's reach. She was so turned on, she could barely breathe.

"Jesus, you drive me crazy," he muttered, pulling her on top of him and taking control of the kiss, working her mouth with an expertise that had them both panting and desperate in record time.

With a speed and grace that shouldn't have surprised her, Max rolled her onto her back and pushed inside her.

His chest grazed her nipples with each stroke of his hips, and she marveled at the strength of him, the way the muscles in his shoulders and arms bulged with effort as he held himself over her, staring into her eyes as he plunged deep, driving her closer and closer to the edge.

And just when she couldn't stand it anymore, Max increased the pressure, lowering himself so that their bodies were flush, pushing her into the mattress as he caught her mouth with his. Her body detonated again under the weight of him, sending shockwave after shockwave radiating through her, leaving her helpless to do anything but hold him close as he joined her in ecstasy.

CHAPTER EIGHTEEN

"I CAN FEEL you thinking," he teased, and Emma snuggled more fully against him. He stroked the pad of his thumb against her arm, and it was one of those perfect moments that Emma had been searching for. She was in the middle of a memory right now, and part of her wanted to hold on to it, not blow it up like she was about to do. But the other part of her knew that she might never get this opportunity again, and so she took a chance.

"Can I ask you something?"

He angled his chin down so their eyes met. "Why do I get the feeling you're going to, regardless of my answer?"

Her smile was guilty, and he chuckled, the sound of it reverberating through his chest. He pressed a kiss against her hair. "Go ahead."

"Kaylee said something about you not taking a salary?"

He went eerily still, just for a moment, withdrawing as though what she'd said was an affront. "It's nothing."

It was his this-matter-is-finished tone of voice.

She'd seen him shut down heated boardroom arguments with it several times, but tonight, after what they'd shared, she refused to be intimidated.

"Considering you spend all your time at the office, it doesn't seem like nothing," she ventured. He might not answer, but she needed to try. She'd shared so much of herself with him, all that stuff about her mom, and now she wanted something in return. A little piece of the enigmatic man who gave the appearance of being cold and aloof. Tonight, he'd made her body burn with his sexual prowess and her heart melt with his kindness. She wanted to know him better.

Max exhaled. "It's a token. An empty promise I made to myself."

It was more than she'd expected, so she raked her fingers through the smattering of hair on his chest, stroking them back and forth in a lazy rhythm, hoping the silence might coax something further from him.

"My father took advantage of…someone I brought to his attention. A man I respected and greatly admired. He was a brilliant software developer. My father blackmailed him, swindled his intellectual property from him and held him hostage with legalities, until he was just a wrecked shell of a man. So wrecked that he broke a decade of sobriety and drove his car into a pole."

Her palm stilled over his heart, poor comfort, but she needed to touch him. Needed him to know she was there. He stared at her hand on his skin, his expression both blank and quizzical, as though he wasn't quite in the present, but he didn't understand how he'd gotten there.

"Max," she said softly.

He shook his head, and his eyes cleared. "There's a local charity that takes care of families who've lost someone to drunk driving. They provide them with therapy, financial assistance, whatever they need, regardless of whether their loved one was the victim or the perpetrator."

"And you donate your salary."

His nod was almost imperceptible. Something about the specificity of the charity made her heart pinch. "Did he have children?"

The words were a long time coming, and they held an edge of pain, as evidenced by the tightness in Max's voice. "A son. Aidan."

"You know him?"

"We were friends. Before I took over Whitfield Industries."

Something about the way he said it warned her pursuing it further would be a dead end.

"I'm so sorry." Beneath her fingers, his muscles relaxed a fraction. With relief that she hadn't pressed the issue? "That's an incredible thing you're doing, supporting that charity in his honor."

He shook his head, rejecting the praise. "It isn't. It doesn't change anything. It certainly doesn't fix anything. But I've already benefitted too much from the misfortune of others."

She'd known Max was special. From the moment she'd met him, he'd seemed capable, in control. But until tonight, she hadn't imagined the depth of his strength. The profundity of his character.

"Don't look at me like that."

"Like what?"

"Like I'm a good man. I'm not, Emma. Don't fool yourself. I'm just like my father."

The idea that he thought he was anything like Charles Whitfield leant heat to her voice. "You're nothing like him."

"I'm *exactly* like him. I put business before everything. My father should be rotting in jail for what he did to John Beckett."

He said it so matter-of-factly that it shocked her. No rage. His voice was even and modulated, as though he were giving her the weather report.

"But instead of turning him in, I blackmailed him into retirement, which at the time, struck me as poetic justice. And I told myself I did it so my sister wouldn't have to deal with the fallout of toppling the only parent who ever gave her the time of day. So that my mother wouldn't have to survive another scandal. But the truth is, I did it so there'd still be a business for me to take over when I kicked his ass out. And worst of all, I betrayed my best friend to do it."

Max shrugged at the summation, a momentary flash of something real peeking out from behind the crack in the armor. "Bringing SecurePay to the world, making sure that John's contribution sees the light of day, is one way I atone for what I've done. Letting Aidan hate me for it is the other."

"Have you ever tried to explain what happened?" Emma asked. "I'm sure if Aidan knew why you—"

"I don't do it for forgiveness, Emma. I made my choice, and I live with it. I don't believe in second chances. Some things can't be fixed."

She felt his retreat, the tightening of his muscles, the emotional distance he was trying to erect between them. Emma knew all too well what it was like to have regrets that ate at you. To face reality when all you wanted to do was curl up in a ball and hide. And part of her wanted to give him the space he obviously needed.

But she didn't. Something in her chest keened at the loss of the honesty of the moment they'd just shared, a moment that transcended all the complications that had happened before it. Right now, they were just two people, not a boss and employee, not the betrayed and the betrayer, just a man and a woman.

And Emma wanted it back, for however briefly it might last.

"Don't leave me yet," she said, not sure if he'd understand what she meant, but desperate to make him. Because she couldn't leave him. Not while he was hurting.

Max had been shouldering too many burdens all by himself for far too long. And while Emma knew he'd reject sympathy, she wanted to give him comfort.

To that end, she tucked closer to his side, wrapping an arm around him in as close an approximation of a hug as she could get from this position, and pressed her lips to his chest, right above his heart.

He went deadly still.

"Emma…" He said her name uncertainly, like he wasn't sure if it was a warning or a plea. She didn't let go, though. She just lay there, hugging him, until the stiffness in his muscles receded. Until she felt his breathing even out beneath her cheek.

Only then did she loosen her grip on him, so she could push up on her elbows and look into his eyes. To see for herself that Max was okay. That he was himself again.

He wasn't. Not exactly. His expression was hard, almost dark, and his gaze searched her face, looking for what, she didn't know.

But when he reached up, the hand that cupped her jaw was gentle. His thumb traced her bottom lip. She sighed at the touch, the soft sound kindling a spark in those enigmatic amber eyes.

And that spark set her body ablaze.

"I can't get enough of you."

His words were gravel. They scraped against her nerve endings, and the sweet thrill of arousal turned insistent. His fingers dug into her hip and he rolled her beneath him, chest heaving as he stared down at her, and what she saw in his face stole her breath.

Before, he'd looked at her with desire, but now he looked at her like he needed her, not just any woman, but *her*.

It was world shaking.

And then he canted his hips and pushed deep, and Emma cried out as she wrapped her arms around him, clinging as tightly as she could, afraid if she didn't, she might be swept away completely.

Emma was too tired to discern more than the vague notion of someone moving around.

She and Max had made love half the night, and she'd slept snuggled against his side. In fact, it was the sudden realization that he wasn't there that woke her in the first place.

"What time is it?" she asked, her voice thick and groggy.

"Too early for you to be up. I was trying not to wake you."

She liked hearing Max's deep baritone in the morning. Knowing he'd spent the night next to her.

"But I told Brennan and Hastings I'd meet them at seven, so I have to leave soon. Sully will come back for you."

She managed a muffled sound of acknowledgment, and reached to steal the other pillow, since Max wasn't using it, but something jabbed her in the forearm. She frowned as she scraped her hair off her face, squinting at the white box. "What's this?"

He glanced over his shoulder as he finished his Windsor knot. "Breakfast."

It was *the* tie, she realized. The one she'd used to bind his wrists the night he'd trusted her with one of his deepest secrets. It looked good on him.

He grabbed his suit jacket from the garment bag on the back of the door and then slid into it. It fit his broad shoulders to perfection.

Who'd have thought it could be so erotic watching a man put clothes *on*?

She pulled the sheet over her breasts, before she sat up against the headboard. "You got breakfast and a suit delivered?"

"That's the point of having money. Getting what you want, when you want it."

She rolled her eyes and grabbed the white bakery box, untying the pretty raffia bow. "I'd be more impressed if your suits weren't right next door. This box is probably full of pillow mints or something," she joked.

Then the white edges of cardboard sprang open, revealing its contents.

Her brow creased as she looked up at the powerful man in the suit that cost more than three-months' rent at her old apartment. "But how?"

"I sent Sully to a little Croatian bakery I found." He slipped his watch onto his left wrist, clasping it with quick, efficient movements.

Her heart lurched against her ribs. And that was before he walked over to the bed, and then pressed a kiss to her forehead as he stole one of the prettily iced *medenjaci* cookies from the box and popped it into his mouth.

He chewed thoughtfully for a moment before swallowing. "These are *really* good." He grabbed two more. "I can see why your dad loved your mom's cookies so much."

The casual mention of her family slayed her.

She didn't like the warmth seeping through her chest.

Because this wasn't lust.

It was suspiciously more like another L word.

The scary one.

And if she was in love with Max, that made everything so much worse.

A knock at the hotel room door made him glance over his shoulder. "That must be housekeeping. I asked them to send someone up to take care of the kitchen."

Max walked over to the dresser to grab his wallet.

"I'll let them in on my way out. See you at work?"

He asked the question like nothing had changed, like her whole world hadn't just slid off its axis.

Emma couldn't make her voice work to lie to him, so she nodded instead.

His answering smile stung like a thousand pin pricks.

She stared after him as he left the room, trying to fix the memory in her brain. In her heart. A perfect moment in time to hold close, to look back on after everything imploded.

Because she had to tell him.

She couldn't keep pretending that she could outrun what she'd done. There was no direction that didn't lead to what was happening right now.

I don't believe in second chances. Some things can't be fixed.

This, she realized, was one of those things. She'd screwed up with Max the minute she'd shaken Charles Whitfield's hand.

Tears slipped down her cheeks at the consequences, and she hugged her knees to her chest.

It took a long time for the tears to stop. Even longer for her to find the strength to crawl out of bed.

Emma retrieved her purse from the decorative chair in the corner, and pushed the bedroom door closed on the sounds of someone doing the dishes.

Max would never forgive her for what she'd done. She'd betrayed him, and he was right: there was no fixing it. But maybe, just maybe, she could give him the second chance he deserved with Aidan. With himself.

Reaching into the zippered pocket in her leather tote, she extracted the burner phone Charles had given her, thumbs flying over the keypad.

The text message read: Grand Park fountain @ noon.

She hit Send.

CHAPTER NINETEEN

"I've taken all your reports into consideration—" along with AJ's, but Max didn't tell that to the men sitting on the other side of his desk "—and I've decided to move forward with releasing SecurePay on Tuesday, as scheduled. I'll expect regular updates in the days leading up to the launch."

Brennan stared at him evenly, saying nothing. Hastings jumped amiably into the silence. "Understood. Gotta keep those shareholders happy. I keep trying to get this guy to take Soteria public—" Jesse thumbed in Brennan's direction "—but he won't bite."

Brennan cut his partner a sidelong glance, and Hastings stopped babbling. "We have people monitoring the security feeds and firewall around the clock, and we'll have updates to you twice daily, starting immediately. If you have any further questions or concerns, feel free to contact either of us, twenty-four-seven."

Max and Brennan stood, and Hastings followed their lead. With a round of handshakes, business was concluded, and Max was on to a second meeting with Vivienne, to fill her in on the morning's results and

make sure that there were no outstanding legal hic-
cups that might throw off the launch.

Then he briefed Kaylee on where things stood
so she was prepared and ready for the day they unleashed SecurePay into the world. As he escorted his
sister out of his office, he decided to see if Emma felt
like joining him for lunch.

He'd been so busy that he hadn't seen her since
that morning, when she'd been sitting in bed with
sleepy eyes and sex-tousled hair, naked under the
sheet clutched to her breasts.

Or better yet, they could skip lunch.

"Sherri, can you get Emma on the phone for me?"

"I haven't seen her today. Jim was looking for her
earlier."

Max frowned. That was strange. He pulled his cell
phone from his inner breast pocket, but she hadn't
texted. He tried calling, and it went straight to voice
mail.

Maybe she was sick. He glanced at his watch. He
could head over to the hotel and check on her before
his afternoon meeting.

"I'll be back at one thirty," he told Sherri, as he
headed for the elevator. "If the marketing department
drops off those proofs of the new campaign I asked
for, just leave them on my desk."

He spent the duration of the descent telling himself that this worry winding though his chest was ridiculous, that she was fine. Sherri might have missed
her arrival, her battery could have died, maybe she'd
used the contact info he'd forced her to take for his
driver, and she was just running an errand…but when

he emerged from the building, Sully was parked in his usual spot.

Damn.

Max strode toward his car, but before he reached it, a slight figure bumped into him, surprising him out of his tunnel vision. He steadied himself. "Are you oka…"

The question died on his lips as recognition hit. The black leather jacket, black jeans, black boots and a black sweatshirt with the hood pulled up, despite the California heat. He was familiar with the game. And the player.

"Jesus, AJ. I'd better still have my wallet."

The woman grinned as she turned to face him, holding out the expensive brown leather. "Gotta keep the skills sharp."

He grabbed it back, tucking it away. "I thought I paid you enough to render those skills extinct."

"Sure you do. But if I forget all the moves, what good am I? I mean, if I can't pick your pocket, I can't finesse my way past your firewall, either. It's all about the dance, you know?"

"I don't have time to dance right now. What are you doing here?"

Her brown eyes turned serious, and Max didn't like the resulting clench in his gut.

"I need to talk to you."

Max glanced back at the building that housed Whitfield Industries. She shouldn't have come here. And he certainly couldn't take her inside.

"Come on."

He gave Sully the signal to stand down, and his

bodyguard and driver lowered his big frame back into the car. Max hurried AJ to the vehicle and followed her inside.

Sully raised the privacy partition as he pulled away from the curb and just started driving, no explanations required. Max made a mental note to increase Sully's bonus.

"Tell me."

"Hello to you, too," she said with an arched eyebrow, pulling the black hood down to reveal her raven curls.

Max returned the rebuke with an unimpressed look.

"Yeah, yeah. I followed the money."

He frowned. "I thought you already did that. You said she checked out."

AJ looked uncomfortable, fidgeting with the drawstring at her neck. It wasn't like her.

"Not Emma's money. Your dad's."

The announcement cold-cocked him.

"Turns out that the place taking care of her mom wasn't just nice—it was really nice. Even the e-transfers with all the zeroes she sent weren't coming close to taking care of the luxury-sized price tag."

"My father."

AJ nodded. "Emma might not be your bad guy on this hack, but she's up to those pretty blue eyes in something shady."

"And you're sure—"

"They're in cahoots? Colluding? In bed together?"

AJ flinched beneath the weight of his glower.

"Whoa. Bad choice of words, I see. Down boy.

That was only meant in the figurative sense. But yeah. I think they're connected. Nobody with your dad's rep fronts several grand a month to a veritable stranger without getting something in return. And I did the math. Until you hired her, there are no links between the two of them, financial or otherwise. Which makes you the common denominator."

Max couldn't help but think back to his father showing up at the office. Charles Whitfield was a charming bastard, brilliant at making people feel comfortable. It was his superpower—make them like him, make them trust him, so they didn't even realize he'd manipulated them until it was too late.

It was how his father had managed to keep Whitfield Industries afloat, even as his stubborn refusal to embrace change had the company falling further and further behind its competitors.

Max had worked his ass off to turn Whitfield Industries back into a financial leader and secure his and Kaylee's birthrights. SecurePay was the crown jewel in his plan, the unmitigated success that would win his board's loyalty once and for all. And convince even those who counted themselves among his father's friends and cronies that Max had what it took to guide the company to greatness, if they were willing to keep up with the times.

And put Charles Whitfield's tainted legacy firmly to rest.

In retrospect, Max realized he should have known something was up. At the time, he hadn't given it a second thought—he'd been too furious that Charles had gained access to his building without him knowing—but his father had never passed up an opportunity to charm a beautiful woman, especially if he could make Max look bad while doing it. Yet that day, his father had blown right past charisma to snake oil salesman…almost like he'd been deliberately trying to make her uncomfortable.

And Emma…

The color had drained from her face when she'd seen Charles. But that had been before she knew what he'd done. Before Max had told her everything.

Betrayal hit hard and fast, a sucker punch to the solar plexus. And if he'd thought it had hurt when he found out what a bastard his father was, if he'd thought pain was his best friend vowing revenge on him, well, those things were nothing compared to this.

"You have proof." It wasn't a question. There was a reason that he'd recruited AJ after Wes had caught her poking around in Whitfield Industries' business. She was one of the best, or she wouldn't be in his car right now.

She tugged an envelope from the pocket of her black jacket.

Max didn't bother to open it, just tucked it in the breast pocket of his suit jacket. The show of trust lit something he couldn't quite name in AJ's brown eyes. "Listen, when I was poking around in your father's finances, there was an echo."

"An echo?"

AJ nodded. "Yeah. Nothing concrete, but something that happens sometimes, when I'm in the zone. I know it sounds a bit woo-woo, but it's like I can sense if I'm following a fresh trail, or if I'm stepping in footprints. And with your father's account, it felt like the latter. Like someone had walked the path before me, you know? I can't explain it any better than that. But I don't think I'm the only one who knows what he did for Emma's mom."

Max tried to absorb the ramifications of that, but he couldn't make sense of it. "I'll keep that in mind. Where can we drop you?"

"Near the park is great. I'll hop out just after the courthouse."

Max rapped on the partition, giving Sully their destination, which was only a block and a half away.

"Before you go…"

"Yeah?"

"Were you planning on giving me my watch back?"

With a long-suffering sigh, she pulled it from her other pocket and handed it back to him. "Fine. I guess I'll just take my bonus in cash. Like usual."

AJ reached for the door handle as the car rolled to a stop, but she hesitated. Looked back at him. Her sudden somberness made the back of his neck prickle with dread.

"Listen, this is total speculation, more gut feeling from watching bad people do bad things, and I wasn't going to tell you until I had eyes on it…but your dad's phone is pinging off a cell tower near here, and when your girl left the hotel today, she grabbed an Uber north…"

Max didn't ask how AJ knew Emma was staying at the hotel. Or that she'd taken an Uber. AJ made it her business to know everything. Which explained the sudden burn of acid in his stomach.

AJ pulled her hood back up as she pushed open the door. "Let's just say that you might want to stick around for a few minutes. Someone tall, blonde and deceitful might be looking for a ride."

The door slammed before Max could fully digest the import of her words.

As he watched AJ head toward the park, she bumped into a familiar figure with a phone to his ear who was standing near a bank of fenced-in palm trees. The man shot her a dirty look before smoothing his suit jacket and striding toward the black town car—almost identical to the one Max sat in now—that slid up to the curb ahead of him. He watched, sick to his stomach, as his father got inside.

Moments later, just as AJ had predicted, a beautiful blonde appeared almost exactly where his father had been moments ago.

His muscles turned to steel as the full weight of her deception sank in, but Max forced himself to open the door, to get out of the car. As though she felt the animosity radiating off him, Emma looked up from her phone, stumbling on her heels when their eyes met.

His words were full of bite.

"Get in. Now."

CHAPTER TWENTY

HE KNEW.

The proof was in the rigid set of his broad shoulders, the depth of betrayal in his amber eyes.

And just like that, the cataclysmic collision course that had been spelled out in their crossed stars was set, about to play out beneath the warmth of the California sun and a cloudless blue sky.

There was relief in not having to outrun it anymore, a resigned sort of peace in not wondering when it would sneak up on her.

There was also a hurt so deep she could barely breathe through the pain, and she hadn't expected it to cut so deep.

But she hadn't expected to fall in love with him, either.

"I said get in." He ground the words from between his teeth.

She couldn't summon any ire at the command. In her sorrow, it struck her as Max being Max. And that's when she realized the missing him had already begun, even though he was standing right in front of her.

"No."

I can't. Please don't make me.

Being alone with him while he hated her was more than she could bear.

His jaw ticked with fury. Emma ignored the impulse to reach up and soften the knotted muscle. Instead, she took her cue from him and set her shoulders.

"I won't insult either of us by telling you I'm sorry for what I've done, because I'm not. Not all the way." She rubbed her right thumb against her mother's ring.

"I did what I had to. I needed the money, and I didn't know you yet, not like now, and the information didn't...never mind. No excuses. I did it, and I had my reasons. Just like you had your reasons for making me stay, right?"

His continued silence served as confirmation.

She nodded, dropped her gaze to the sidewalk beneath her pumps. When she looked up again, her smile was sad. "Only a fool would rehire the prime suspect in a security breach, and you're a lot of things, Max, but you're not a fool."

His jaw flexed. "I'm not doing this on the street."

"I'm not doing *this* at all," she said simply.

It's already done.

Emma wondered for a moment if the entire world had run out of air, or if it was just her lungs that the oxygen had abandoned.

There was pain in his eyes, in his voice, and he let her see all of it.

"I *trusted* you."

Her heart shattered into jagged shards that cut her chest with each breath.

"I know."

It had meant everything to have him share those broken pieces of himself with her. To share her sadness with him, too.

Being with Max had helped her find herself again. The Emma she was before her mother had gotten sick, the Emma she wanted to be going forward.

Even if she had to go forward without him.

Her gaze dropped to the hand that was strangling his tie.

The tie.

Her own hand flexed at the phantom sensation of his fingers entwined with hers.

He dropped it suddenly, snatching his hand back as though the silk had burned him. As though she had.

The ravaged look on his face tore at her guts. He tipped his head back. Closed his eyes.

She could see where he'd nicked himself shaving on the underside of his jaw, near his chin.

Then he smoothed the mangled silk with economical, precise movements. Restoring order. Setting things right.

She was losing him.

When he lowered his head, he was the picture of icily reserved detachment. His amber eyes were flat, controlled, staring through her as though they were complete strangers.

It was always going to end like this.

The reminder didn't keep her hands from shaking, but she rallied as best she could, shoving her emotions back down to the pit of her stomach and locking them away.

"It's nothing personal, Max. Isn't that what you said?"

His nod was almost imperceptible. If she wasn't staring at him like he was her whole world, she might have missed it.

"Just business."

She'd fucked up so bad. She loved him so much.

"Just business," she repeated.

"I think this is understood," Max said, his voice devoid of any particular inflection, "but in case it wasn't clear, you're fired, effective immediately."

Everything inside her shattered.

"Perfectly clear."

Walk away. Just walk away.

Standing here wishing things were different was a waste of time, she reminded herself. And Max hated having his time wasted.

"Goodbye, Max."

Something flickered in his eyes. A beat slipped by, when he should have spoken, but he didn't. Hope pricked her heart. And then…

"Goodbye, Emma."

She needed to go. Her heels clicked against the sidewalk as she forced herself to move, to walk blindly forward, to get the fuck away from him.

Everything in her hurt.

When a cab pulled up to let someone out at the courthouse, she crawled in.

"Where to, ma'am?"

"Berkshire Suites, please. And then to the airport."

She wasn't sure when the tears had begun streaming down her face, but she hoped to God that Max hadn't seen them.

It had been a hell of a day.

All he wanted was to go home, pour himself a glass of Scotch, and then another, and forget he'd ever laid eyes on Emma Mathison.

But before that could happen, he needed Vivienne Grant to get the hell out of his office.

"She's in breach of contract. You can sue the shit out of her."

Max shot her a cutting look. "I want this over and done. Just run it as though she resigned. Make sure she gets paid out as per the original agreement."

"Minus the inconvenience bonus you tacked on?" Vivienne asked, looking up from her notes.

"Including the inconvenience bonus."

He didn't like the judgmental look she gave him.

"You're my lawyer, Vivienne. Not my executioner."

"You want to pay Emma big bucks to not do her job, that's your business. I just point out your legal options and do what I'm told," she countered, and the picture she'd just painted of herself as a docile, order-following lamb was so far from the reality of his ball-busting attorney that it brought a ghost of a smile to his lips, despite his sour mood.

"And that's why I pay *you* the big bucks," he reminded her.

She nodded in a gesture that he might have described as distracted if she weren't looking at him with such intensity. Then her gaze dropped to his chest, and when he followed it, he found his hand was clenched around his fucking tie again.

The one Emma had used that night.

The night he'd given up control, given her control.

The night that would haunt him for the rest of his life.

Disgusted, he yanked the knot loose and pulled the strip of material from beneath his collar, balling it up and tossing it in the general vicinity of the waste basket beside his desk.

Vivienne raised her eyebrows at the atypical display. "What did that tie ever do to you?"

Besides fuck him in every way possible? Max thought darkly. He popped the top button, so his shirt would stop strangling him.

"Just make this all go away," he ordered, signing the documents in front of him before handing them to her.

She tucked them on top of her legal pad as she stood. "I'm sorry she's gone. I liked her," Vivienne said softly, but she'd already turned on her heel and left before Max could process the uncharacteristic evidence of his lawyer's humanity.

He leaned back in his chair.

The ghost of Emma was all over his office. The comfort of her cheek against his chest after his father's impromptu visit. The clash of their bodies when he'd shoved her up against the window and torn her skirt.

His desk.

Max swore under his breath and tossed the pen

he'd used to sign Vivienne's documents on top of the speech notes Kaylee had left for him to review before the launch.

Emma had betrayed him with a man he despised, and he was sitting here like a lovesick cuck, remembering her hands on his body.

Get your head in the game, Whitfield.

She'd lied to him. The entire time she'd worked for him. The entire time they were fucking. Even last night, when things had been…different.

At least for him it had been.

His father's voice was in his brain.

You're soft. That's your problem. You care too much.

Well, now she was gone. For good.

Problem solved.

Max stood. He needed to move. He needed to go home. He needed that drink.

As he rounded the side of his desk, his gaze snagged on the limp carcass of his tie. The skinny end of the black and gray material was draped over the side of the waste basket, but the thick end lay unfurled across the carpeting like an abandoned snakeskin.

He grabbed it and shoved it in his pocket as he headed for the door.

CHAPTER TWENTY-ONE

"WELCOME HOME, MR. WHITFIELD."

Max nodded to the concierge but kept his pace through the lobby quick. He wasn't in the mood for small talk.

"Ms. Mathison left something for you, sir."

Her name echoed like a gunshot in his brain, stopping him. "Is she here?"

Gerald shook his head. "She left earlier this afternoon in a taxi. I'm afraid I haven't seen her since, nor did she inform me of her destination, though she had her suitcase with her. And if I may say so, sir, she seemed…upset."

The concierge looked at him expectantly.

"You said you have something for me?"

"Oh, yes. Of course, sir."

Max told himself he didn't care how she'd seemed as he waited for the man to round the reception desk and hand him a beat-up shoebox.

"Don't forget this." Gerald grabbed the manila envelope he'd tucked under his arm and set it on the lid. The way it was torn open struck Max as familiar, and he realized it was the same envelope from the day before. In his office. The one Emma had been carrying after she'd walked his father down to the lobby. Only now it said his name in her elegant, slanted handwriting.

Max's fingers flexed against the cardboard as he headed for the elevator, carefully holding the package in front of him with both hands, keeping it straight and still, like he was holding a bomb.

He stared at the ripped edge of the envelope as he pushed the up button. Its contents had shifted slightly when Gerald had handed it over, and the edge of a photo peeked out, confirming his suspicions.

Oh, it was going to detonate all right.

When he arrived on the top floor, Max made a point of keeping his eyes forward, heading straight to his door, not giving into the absurd desire to go to her room and confirm Gerald's report. To see for himself that she was really gone.

Max walked into his suite, abandoning the package on the coffee table as he passed it, not stopping until he arrived at the bar cart so he could pour himself that glass of Scotch.

He drained it in one go, topped it up and took this round over to the sofa with him. Max sat on the middle cushion, his legs spread wide. With a contemplative sip, he stared at the envelope with his name on the front.

She was a consummate liar. He shouldn't give a damn what she'd left for him. And even as he told himself that, he leaned forward, set his drink on the edge of the glass table and grabbed the envelope.

Tipping the contents into his hand, he revealed

a stack of images printed on letter-sized paper. He flipped through the photos—candid shots of Emma and his father, a little grainy from the printer, but in focus, with a small time and date stamp in the bottom right corner of each. They were obviously taken with a zoom lens, by some PI his father had paid to document each meeting, no doubt.

"Leverage is the key to any good negotiation," he'd always said.

Bastard.

Reminding himself to breathe, he continued with the bittersweet torture. About half-way through the stack, the pain of seeing them together started to dull, and he found himself focusing solely on Emma, watching her betray him, again and again, in an assortment of outfits on a dozen different days.

She was beautiful. Even as she handed papers full of secrets to the man who wanted to ruin him. Even when he was trying to hate her for her treachery. Even when he hated himself for not being able to.

Max dropped the photos on the cushion beside him and leaned forward. Took a drink.

What the hell was wrong with him?

He rested his elbows on his thighs, pressing the glass to his cheek.

This was madness.

He took the last bracing gulp of his Scotch, and exchanged the empty glass for the shoebox, setting it in his lap.

Just like ripping off a Band-Aid, he told himself, and flicked open the lid.

Inside was a phone and a stack of papers.

He pressed the power button on the phone, and while it started up, he sorted through the rest.

Judging by the dates Emma had handwritten at the top—each of which corresponded to one of the date stamps on the pictures—they'd met quarterly for the last three years. But as he scanned through the photocopied reports on Whitfield Industries letterhead, detailing the progress of the project, his frown deepened.

Max had eaten, slept and breathed SecurePay for so long that it was easy for him to discern how incomplete the information was without comparing these documents to the originals. Large swaths of data were missing, and key dates had been changed, rendering them largely useless.

Emma had actually done a brilliant job of giving his father just enough real info to keep him from realizing how little he was getting. Luckily, Charles Whitfield was a proud Luddite, or Emma might never have gotten away with this.

Still, he thought uncharitably, nothing here proved blackmail. It was a bunch of shoddy reports about SecurePay, and some pictures of the two of them together. Hardly a smoking gun.

Idly, he grabbed the phone and scrolled through the texts. They reached back the full three years that he'd known her. Sparsely worded messages that consisted mostly of times, dates and locations, nothing to prove the identity of either sender, except for Emma's word. And Emma was gone.

Though he supposed the texts combined with the

dated surveillance photos and reports might line up in a way that proved his father was on the other end of the communication. If they could find his phone…

His thumb hovered over the screen as he got to the end of the messages.

The most recent text was dated this morning.

The morning after he'd carried her from the kitchen to the bedroom, and she'd touched and caressed his body with such tenderness that it had almost undone him.

The same morning he'd woken Sully at five to track down Croatian gingerbread, just to see her smile.

Thirty minutes after he'd left for work and realized he'd fallen in love with her.

Grand Park fountain @ noon.

That was it.

Four words and an @ symbol were the catalyst that had changed his world irreparably.

Max closed the text window with every intention of tossing the phone back in the box, but the sight of the voice recording app—the lone icon at the top of the home screen—stayed his hand.

Leaning back against the couch, he opened the program and hit Play.

The sounds of the park were tinny in the speaker—the muted shouts and laughter of people, the rush of the fountain as water slapped against the pavement—and then he heard his father's voice.

"Emma. I was pleased to get your message this morning."

Her laugh was bitter. "Well now. I've pleased Charles Whitfield. I can die happy." Though sarcasm dripped through the speaker, Max realized she'd just managed to confirm his father's identity on the recording.

"I was concerned after our time together yesterday that you might try to...*dissolve* our working relationship."

"I considered it, but you've made sure I'm trapped."

"It's good that you've finally realized that."

The joyous shrieks of children playing took over the audio for a moment before he could hear Emma's voice again.

"—this ridiculous plan to frame Max for insider trading will never work, don't you?"

"You underestimate me, my dear. I've been manipulating Max for his entire life. I'm quite adept at this point. Just look at you. Your mother's been dead for six months now, and I'm still holding her over your head."

Max's fists tightened at his father's jab, not the one at him, which was no more than he expected, but at Emma. Especially when she stayed quiet for a few beats after the verbal blow.

When she spoke again, her voice was low and dangerous. "I took your money and gave you information on SecurePay so that my mother would have the best care available, but don't you ever mention her to me again. You're not fit to speak of her."

His chest swelled with pride, not just for her return jab, but her ingenuity, too, as she established the parameters of the blackmail for the record.

But her next words felled him.

"Your son is twice the man you are! And tonight I'm going to tell him everything you've done. Everything I've done. And I don't care what you do in return. So go ahead and unleash your debt collectors. I'll file for bankruptcy if I have to, but I'm not going to let you hurt him anymore."

"My God. You're in love with him, aren't you?"

His father's question beat in Max's chest, pummeling his ribs from the inside.

"How trite. Maybe I should have chosen Farnsworth as my inside man after all. At least he wouldn't have been such a handful.

"Here's something you obviously don't know about Max. He will never forgive you for your betrayal. You're so sure he'll let you pour your guts out to him? The second he realizes you've been in contact with me for the last three years, he'll stop listening. Cut you out of his life with the precision of a master surgeon. You think I ruined his relationship with his sister? With his best friend? I just waited. He did it himself."

Even sitting, the punch landed with enough force to make him stagger. Max's hand tightened on the phone until it cut into his palm.

"You might love him, but he is incapable of returning that particular emotion. He's just like me. And when push comes to shove, he'll put Whitfield Industries first. Just like I taught him."

"You're wrong! Max is nothing like you. He cared about John Beckett. And he still cares about Kay-

lee. About Aidan. He might have made some mistakes, but he's spent his entire life trying to make
up for them, trying to do the right thing. You think
you know him, but you don't. Not like I do. He's—"

Max paused the audio. He couldn't listen anymore.
Shame ate at him, And the fact that she would still
defend him, after everything he'd told her, after everything he'd done to her.

He'd blackmailed her. Doubted her. Lied to her.

He had no right to sit here and listen to her praise
him now. Not when he'd done nothing but live down
to his father's expectations of him. Not when he'd
let her walk out of his life without putting up a fight.

Hell, he'd ordered her to leave him.

Max tossed the phone back in the shoebox, but
when he started loading the rest of the documents, a
Post-it stuck to the cardboard caught his eye.

Her pretty writing wrung his heart.

If you're reading this, then you got to the bottom of the box, and now you know everything.
Well, everything except that I never meant to
hurt you.

And Max? You're not like him. You're better than him.
Emma

He didn't believe in second chances. And in the
most humbling moment of his life, he found that
Emma had all but gift wrapped one for him.

He just had to accept it.

The realization settled into his bones, made him feel solid as he formulated his plan of attack.

Tonight, he was going to finish getting all the way drunk.

And tomorrow, he was going to make a phone call.

CHAPTER TWENTY-TWO

FOUR DAYS LATER, the results of that phone call were about to take effect, and Max was not looking forward to any of it.

"Where the hell have you been? I've been calling you all morning!"

He hadn't taken three steps into his office before his sister was on him, shoving speech notes in his hands and talking far too loudly.

"You look like shit. Jesus, Max. Are you hungover? That's just great. I would tell you how incredibly stupid that is, but it will have to wait until later, because right now you need to straighten your tie and get downstairs for the press conference. We're thirty minutes out, and we've got a thousand details to go over."

Well, here goes nothing.

"We're not launching."

His sister went still at the pronouncement. "You're joking, right?"

Max gave a curt shake of his head, prepping for the tirade Kaylee was about to unleash on him, judging by the flare of her nostrils and the clench of her jaw.

Not that he blamed her. This was the one part of the plan that he'd been dreading above all else.

"And you're telling me this *now*? Half an hour before the packed auditorium of tech geeks and journalists are expecting you to blow their collective minds? You, the man who worships on the altar of 'it's all about timing,' are canceling a product launch at the last minute and—"

He lost track of her grievances in the buzz that was building in his head, drowning out the diatribe he knew he deserved. But she was wrong if she thought he hadn't planned out what was happening right now to the second. In fact, all he'd thought about for the last four days was *timing*…

That's what had been bothering him since the spyware had been discovered on Emma's computer.

This launch was everything, the focus of his business life for the last five years, and the idea that got him out of bed every morning for the last seven. He'd dedicated a large amount of resources to it, and if it flopped, it would be catastrophic.

But despite the reassurances he'd received from his cybersecurity team, Max couldn't get rid of the doubt that had attached itself to the base of his spine like a parasite.

There was an internal hack. On Emma's computer. Emma, who had already quit.

When his father wanted to manipulate him, he'd gone old-school—found a plant on the inside. Hacking wouldn't have even occurred to Charles Whitfield. And it was almost inconceivable that it was strictly by chance that Emma, his father's spy, would also end up the one targeted to be the fall guy for this hack.

Separately, it was a pain in the ass. But all those aspects converging just as they were preparing to launch struck him as too much of a coincidence.

An echo, AJ had said. *Like someone had walked the path before me, you know?*

Something was off. Something that, if it got out, could bury SecurePay for good. He should have noticed sooner, but he'd been too focused on proving himself. To his father. To Aidan. To the world.

The fact that all the decrypted code seemed to be worthless didn't soothe Max's unease. It just made him feel like he was being lulled into a false sense of security, so he'd continue with his plan to release SecurePay on schedule.

Something bad was coming if he went through with it. He knew it, despite the security reports. Despite AJ's intel. He felt it in his gut.

Emma was wrong. He *was* just like his father. He'd blackmailed her into staying at Whitfield Industries against her will and justified it to himself because it was for the good of the company. But if he pushed SecurePay through now, regardless of the breach, it wasn't just his ego on the line. It was his company's reputation. He'd covered up his father's sins for that very reason five years ago.

But Emma was right, too—he didn't have to be like Charles Whitfield. He could do better. He could do the right thing before it was too late.

"We're not launching," he repeated, breaking into his sister's ongoing polemic when she paused for a breath. "We need to come clean about the security breach. I'm not putting SecurePay on the market until we figure out who's behind the hack."

Kaylee shook her head at the proclamation, not in protest, but in resignation. She had always been able to recognize when his mind was made up and nothing was going to sway him anymore. Even back when they were kids.

"This is going to be a PR nightmare, not to mention a financial one," Kaylee warned.

He knew it. God, did he know it.

"Yeah, well, get ready to earn your money."

She frowned. "It's not me I'm worried about. As it happens, I'm really good at my job, Max. You're the one who has to stand in the middle of the lion's den and throw the red meat."

Okay, he amended. Maybe *this* part of the plan was going to be worse.

Concealing his flinch, he shook his head. "Actually, I've got a meeting that I need to get to, so I'm going to need you to handle this."

He took in Kaylee's shell-shocked expression.

And in that moment, he wanted nothing more than to confide in his sister. Hug her. Something.

But he couldn't. Because if the purpose of his meeting leaked ahead of time, the last four days, the last five years, everything he'd risked on this project, would be for nothing. So he hid behind his usual brusque autocracy, hoping he hadn't already tipped her off with the out-of-character display.

"You're fully capable of making up a statement for the media and pretending I told you to say it. You've done it plenty of times before. And make sure you push home the fact that SecurePay isn't dead. It's just postponed until we get to the bottom of the hack."

Besides, he added silently. *By this afternoon, no one's going to be dwelling on the SecurePay postponement anyway.*

"You asshole!" The epithet ricocheted through the quiet of his office. He'd never seen Kaylee so worked up. "You expect me to believe that not only are you euthanizing your life's work on a whim, but you've managed to double-book yourself for the funeral, too?"

His voice was resigned. "If there was any other way, I swear to you I'd take it, Kale."

The childhood nickname felt rusty on his tongue. He'd stopped calling her that when he was twelve years old. When he'd cut her out, just like his father had wanted him to. Hearing it now brought color to her cheeks.

"Don't you dare call me that!" she hissed.

She grabbed the forgotten speech notes from his hand and looked him straight in the eye. "I quit."

Max frowned. "You don't mean that."

"Consider this my three-weeks' notice. Right now, I'm going to go out there and handle this for you, because that's my job. But I'm done giving everything to the family business, when most of the time, I don't even feel like part of the family.

"I have spent the last five years working my ass off for you, big brother. Trying to prove myself to you, and after all this time, you don't even have enough respect for me to tell me what the hell is going on?"

Max flinched at the assessment. "Kaylee…"

"Don't. I don't want to hear it. When I'm done kicking ass in the lions' den, I'll type up my resignation letter and leave it on your desk. Now, get out of my way."

And with that, his little sister turned and walked out the door, toward the press conference he'd just blown up on purpose.

Max considered going after her. He wanted to, even though he knew there was nothing he could do right now. Nothing he could say.

Besides, he'd watched enough flare-ups between her and his mother to know that when things got bad, Kaylee needed some time to cool off.

He'd call her tomorrow and set things right. When he could tell her everything.

Rounding his desk, Max opened the locked drawer and retrieved the phone from his safe. As he tucked it in his pocket his eyes lighted on the steel statue he kept on the edge of his desk. He reached out and traced the sharp edges of the flames that made up the horse's mane.

"I'm sorry, John. I'm going to make this up to you." The apology was no more than a whisper.

Then he set his jaw and walked out of his office. There would be time for self-recrimination later, but right now, he had somewhere to be.

CHAPTER TWENTY-THREE

MAX'S HEAD ACHED, but he couldn't be sure if it was the result of his overindulgence for the last four nights, the way his fight with Kaylee was still ringing in his ears, or the fact that Sully was pulling up to the cold stone fortress that was Max's childhood home.

He hated coming back here under any circumstances, but this visit was going to be particularly rough. With a curt knock on the door, Max braced himself for what lay ahead.

The dignified, balding man dressed smartly in a navy suit who opened the door was just one more ridiculous way his mother tried to prove that the Whitfields were both rich and dignified. The farce was almost too much to bear. Especially today.

"Where is my father, Newsome?"

"In his study."

Max stepped past him. "No need to escort me. I remember the way."

He barely looked at the posh interior, with its intricate pillars and its eighteen-foot ceilings. The familiar luxury was beneath his notice, as was the cream decor with blue accents favored by his mother that went through a multitude of tweaks each season. He'd long ago given up trying to keep abreast of his mother's penchant for redesign whenever the mood struck.

"Max? What a surprise."

As though he'd summoned her with his thoughts, his mother appeared at the top of the staircase in pearls and a Chanel suit, her plastic smile radiating tolerance tinged with reproach. He waited dutifully as she descended the steps.

"We weren't expecting you."

He accepted his mother's air kiss.

"But I suppose at least one of my children makes an effort."

Max had long ago accepted the fact that Charles and Sylvia Whitfield were flawed, power-hungry people who cared nothing for anyone beyond themselves. But for God's sake, Kaylee wasn't even here, and still his mother couldn't resist taking a swipe.

"I'd love to stay and chat, but I'm up to my neck in fabric swatches, and I have a million decisions to make before the interior designer arrives. Next time you're coming, be a dear and make an appointment with my assistant so that we can have a real conversation."

She didn't wait for a response before disappearing down the hall. Not that it mattered to Max. He turned and headed straight for his father's ornate mahogany office in the back of the house.

"You goddamn son-of-a-bitch."

The slur barely fazed his father, who was pouring himself an afternoon bourbon.

"Max. To what do I owe the pleasure?"

"Emma told me everything."

His father raised an imperious brow. "Well, well, well. I thought there was something between the two of you in the boardroom that day, but I didn't realize it was so…serious."

The fact that his father didn't even need to ask what he was talking about pushed Max to the limits of his patience, but he fought the urge to lash out, reminding himself again why he was here.

He schooled his features back into his customary bland expression. He would not give his father the satisfaction.

"Not that I blame you. She's a beautiful woman. Smart, too. But everyone has a chink in the armor. Unlike you, family is very important to her. She would have done anything to help her poor, dying mother. I snared her much more easily than expected. Luckily, her mother took quite a downturn not long after she started working for you, so it made her easy pickings."

His father took a sip of his liquor.

"Which was fortunate for me, because my next choice for informant was Gordon Farnsworth. The man loves to bet on the ponies. In fact, you should probably keep an eye on him. But he's not nearly as easy on the eyes as Emma, wouldn't you agree?"

"Don't you dare say her name," Max ordered, and his father looked taken aback by the venomous tone.

"Touchy subject, I see. Although if you already know the tale, I suppose I can understand your anger. It wouldn't do to have the CEO of Whitfield Industries fucking the woman who helped him commit insider trading for so many family friends, now would it?"

Max walked over to the bar and poured himself a twelve-year-old Scotch from his father's impressive collection. Hair of the dog. "So that's your game? Frame me for insider trading? Blackmail me into giving you whatever it is you're angling for, just like you've done to every person unfortunate enough to get in your way?"

The memories of what had happened to John Beckett rushed in, flooding his brain, and for the millionth time, Max wished he'd never mentioned the idea of SecurePay to his father back then, let alone John's tech brilliance.

And the worst part was, Charles hadn't had any intention of moving forward with SecurePay. He'd just bound John Beckett in legalese so that no one else could get their hands on the promising first steps he was making, or the patents he held.

Half the reason that Max had been so dogged in his quest to make SecurePay a success was to ensure John hadn't died in vain. That his legacy would live on. So he could show Aidan that his father's life had amounted to something. And once again, his father had found a way to ruin everything.

"That's one option. But I'd prefer if you just announced at the next board meeting that I'm coming out of retirement." Charles took a seat behind his ornately carved desk, some ostentatious remnant of the 1800s that he was inordinately proud of. "You and I can build Whitfield Industries together. Like we used to."

Max took a large swallow of good Scotch. "Go to hell."

"What are you going to do, son. *Report* me?" He sneered the words. "You didn't do it when that fool Beckett drank himself into a stupor and wrapped himself around a pole, because you were too weak. You could have outed me for blackmail then, but you didn't, because you cared more about Aidan's feelings than you did about vengeance against me."

Max nodded. "You're damn right I did. Because unlike me, Aidan worships his father. And I didn't want him to have to deal with the fallout of John's mistake, a mistake that would never have come to light if you hadn't sent out your low-life spies to pick apart his life just so you get enough leverage to use him like a puppet."

"People always think money is the goal, but it's not. Power is the goal, son. Without power, you have nothing. You never understood that, no matter how many times I tried to teach you that. It's how I know you're not cut out for business. You refuse to see how cutthroat it is. You're too soft."

"If that's how you feel, why do you want back in so badly?"

"SecurePay is so much more than I expected when you pitched it to me back in the day. The world has changed so much in my lifetime, and I realize now that you were right to keep an eye to the future. But as I told Emma when I recruited her, you still need me. You make unnecessary mistakes. In fact, you've made the most rudimentary error of all—dallying with the help is the road to ruin."

Max's hand clenched around his glass at the smear on Emma, the way his father spoke of her like she was nothing more than his plaything. Like she hadn't played an integral part in getting SecurePay ready for market.

"How much? How much did you pay her to ruin her life? And gain leverage over me?"

"Over the last three years? Almost three hundred thousand dollars."

Max pulled out his phone and tapped through to his banking app so he could transfer the money. "There. Consider her debt paid. Your business with Emma Mathison is done. Don't so much as glance in her direction ever again. Do I make myself clear?"

Charles shook his head. "My God. I gave you more credit than that."

"Than what?"

"Than falling for her. I mean, she's beautiful. I'll give you that. But I always thought you were a master of separating business and pleasure. When you chose Whitfield Industries over avenging Beckett's death, over his son's friendship, I thought I'd raised a warrior. But now a pretty face has turned you into a lovesick fool. Don't you understand? I already have what I needed from her."

His father's smarmy chuckle slithered across Max's skin.

"I believe this is the part where you concede gracefully."

Max took a step forward and looked his father right in the eye. "I regret every day that I didn't take you down for what you did to John Beckett. And if the information you have on him wouldn't wreak havoc on Aidan's life, I would do it right now. But I'm not bringing you back in to Whitfield Industries. Not ever. Because you made a mistake, too, in underestimating the lengths I'm willing to go to destroy you."

"A fine show of spine, son, but it's too late. If you don't welcome me back from retirement with open arms and a big smile for the camera, then I'm going straight to the Feds."

Max finished his drink and banged the glass onto the formidable, but ugly, desk. "Well, you're half right."

When Max walked out of his parents' mansion, it was to find the raiding party of FBI agents ready to finish what he'd begun. He stepped out of their way as they poured into his father's house through the door he'd left open.

Better late than never, Max thought, letting his thoughts drift to John Beckett. Thanks to Emma, he'd managed to avenge his tech mentor's death without having to reveal John's secret to Aidan. And just like that, the burden he'd been carrying for the last five years felt lighter.

He let the peace that came from doing the right thing wash over him as one of the agents stepped up to divest him of the wire they'd outfitted him with earlier.

"Mr. Whitfield? If you'll just wait, we'll have some questions for you when this is over."

"Send them through my attorney. I have somewhere else to be."

Walking past the bevy of nondescript vehicles to

the end of the driveway where Sully was waiting for him, Max got into his town car.

"Back to the hotel?"

Max nodded. It was as good a destination as any, because he needed to find Emma, and he had absolutely no idea where to start looking.

Luckily, he knew someone who could help.

AJ's face filled the phone screen, but before he could open his mouth, she was already talking. "If you're calling to see if I got my thank-you money for helping to take down daddy dearest, then every single beautiful penny was accounted for and deposited, and I thank you for your prompt payment. It's a pleasure doing business with you."

"I need to find Emma."

To his surprise, she didn't admonish him for his dictatorial tone like she usually did whenever he skipped the social niceties. She just nodded.

"Since unlike you, I actually care about the environment, I forewent the charter and took the liberty of booking you a first-class ticket instead. I pushed everything to your phone—check-in information, car service, travel itinerary."

As if on cue, his other phone began buzzing frantically within the breast pocket of his suit jacket.

"Emma's staying at some gross, one-star hotel, so when you find her, definitely suggest going back to your place. I'm telling you, when she sees the suite I booked you, you are totally getting laid. It's that nice."

Max scowled at her, his mind running through the number of privacy breaches she would have had to commit to make all that happen, but she just shrugged.

"Ninja, remember?"

Oh, he remembered all right.

AJ made a production of glancing at her empty wrist, miming checking the time. "You'd better get a move on, too. You have just over two hours to pack and clear security, because honestly, I expected this call at least an hour ago. This girl's really thrown off your game."

"We'll talk about your tendency to overstep when I get back."

AJ flicked the warning aside. "Like you're going to remember to be annoyed with me by then. Your return tickets aren't for another ten days. Have fun. Send pictures. I don't want to see you in a suit until you're back on American soil. Oh! And don't forget your passport. Side note, I didn't know your middle name was—"

Max disconnected the call before he shoved the phone back into his jacket as Sully navigated the afternoon traffic that stood between him and his destination.

CHAPTER TWENTY-FOUR

RED ROOFS, GREEN TREES, azure water—Dubrovnik was a visual feast of colors. Emma strolled along the most beautiful pebble beach, the rocks warm and smooth beneath her feet, amidst the sounds of lapping water and happy people frolicking under the warm Croatian sun, willing herself not to succumb to the misery that dogged her every step.

Some trip of a lifetime this was turning out to be.

She sighed. Maybe a drink would help.

Angling herself away from the beach chairs and farther up the shore, she headed for the nearest beachfront bar.

"Um...*jeden* piña colada. *Mosim.*"

The bartender smiled kindly, despite her pitiful attempt at Croatian.

"Make it two."

The sound of his voice hit her like a stun gun, freezing her in place, her synapses stuttering as her brain tried to make sense of what was happening.

Max.

Max was here.

He reached past her and set a few bills of colorful Croatian *kuna* beside her arm.

The barkeep's smile grew wider. "Right away, sir," he said in perfect English as he swept the money from the counter.

Emma had spent her first four days in Dubrovnik sobbing in her cramped, dingy room at the budget hotel, binging on self-pity and *medenjaci* cookies.

It would just figure that he would show up today, during her first foray into the world where she didn't feel like she was undergoing open heart surgery with no anesthetic, to rip open the wounds she'd worked so hard to stitch back up.

And it would just figure that her eyes prickled with overwhelming relief that he had.

Emma drew her first easy breath in five days.

When she turned around to confirm that she wasn't in the midst of a hallucination, he was much closer than she'd expected. Not crowding her so much as filling up space with his presence.

Her nipples tingled to attention at the sight of him, the familiarity of his nearness. Her teal bathing suit did nothing to hide her body's reaction.

Stupid bikini.

In her body's defense, Max was hard to resist when he was fully dressed in a suit. But Max in nothing but red boardshorts and Ray-Bans, his damp hair pushed back from his forehead? It took everything she had not to throw herself in his arms.

She turned back to the bar, rested her elbows on the scarred wood. "What are you doing here?"

"I'm on the lam, actually."

He mimicked her position against the counte

"Well," she said lightly, forcing herself to m
his conversational tone, "it sounds like you cam
the right place. I understand there are no extradi
laws here."

His mouth pulled up in a hint of a smile and
knees went weak. She took a deep, steadying bre
"So why are you running?"

"Because my board of directors is pissed th
pulled the plug on the SecurePay launch at the
minute."

The announcement caught her by surprise, and
turned to look at him. The ache in her chest retur
but this time it was in solidarity with him, and she
better able to bear the hurt. He must be devastat

"And because Kaylee is *definitely* pissed th
made her clean up the mess all by herself, so I c
go have my father arrested for felony blackmail.

Oh, God. Emma sucked in a breath as he pus
his sunglasses up into his hair and met her eyes.

"And while this is pure speculation, I would in
ine the FBI is *probably* pissed that I left the cou
while they were in the middle of raiding his hou

She didn't realize that she'd reached for him
her hand made contact with his forearm, an atte
to comfort him over the tumultuous events he'd t
to pass off in a joking tone.

"I'm so sorry, Max." Not for Charles. He
served what he got. But he was Max's father,
that couldn't have been an easy choice, even a
everything he'd done.

His gaze dropped to her fingers on his skin,

when he looked up again, there was nothing light or jokey about him.

"I know who my father is. He's a manipulator. He plays people and makes money off it, and he doesn't give a damn that he's destroying people's lives in the process. And I can't tell you how sorry I am for what he did to you, using your mother as leverage like that."

Max dropped his head. "But none of that's really why I'm here." The confession was soft. "I'm actually looking for something."

"Oh?" Emma swallowed against the fizzy feeling under her skin, like her blood had been replaced with champagne. "Well, if it's *medenjaci* cookies, you might be too late. That's pretty much all I've eaten since I got here."

"Not cookies," he said, quelling her attempt to hit the release valve. "A second chance."

Her body quaked with the most sublime mixture of fear and optimism. "You're a long way from home for someone who doesn't believe in second chances."

"I'd say I'm exactly where I should be for a man who believes in love."

The words detonated around her like a bomb, and she couldn't breathe through the emotional shrapnel.

"You love me?" she asked shakily, hating the hope that twined through her heart. After everything she'd done, everything he'd done, she'd never let herself wish for this moment. And yet…

"Don't pretend you don't know there's something special between us." He pushed away from the bar.

Stood tall as he turned to face her. "You say you're
about taking chances, making memories. So prove i

Emma gestured around her at the beach, at D
brovnik in general. "I'm here, aren't I?"

"A pretty vacation isn't taking a chance. It's ru
ning away. Taking a risk when you don't have to de
with the consequences isn't taking a risk at all."

Max stepped closer, and she swore, despite t
warmth of the beach-scented air, that she could fe
his body heat, even though he wasn't touching h
She kept her eyes straight ahead, staring at the tann
column of his neck.

Ever so gently, he tucked his finger beneath h
chin and lifted her face until their eyes met, and wh
she saw in those amber depths made her knees wea

"Come back with me."

Something warm unfurled in her chest, replaci
the guilt and sadness of the last few years with
the love she felt for this beautiful, complicated m
who'd flown across an ocean to find her.

"Always so bossy," she chided, her dawning sm
wobbling on her lips. "You can't just order me
leave. No extradition laws, remember?"

"Then I'm asking. I'm asking you to take a chan
with me, Emma. To build memories with me. I lo
you, and I want you in my life."

Everything inside her broke open at the words.

"God, Max. I love you so much." She was alrea
wrapping her arms around his neck, lifting onto h
toes, as the words spilled from her lips a split-seco
before her mouth met his.

His arms closed around her with stunning force, pulling her against him like he never wanted to let go.

She didn't want him to.

It was heaven, being skin-to-skin with Max again, her breasts crushed against his unyielding chest as the sweet thrill of arousal loosened her limbs.

She'd missed this. Him.

She moaned in protest when he pulled away. He was breathing heavily as he leaned his forehead to hers.

"Emma?"

"Yeah?"

"We're about forty-five seconds away from me violating any number of public indecency laws."

She pressed tighter against the evidence of his claim, wringing a groan from him. His fingers dug into her hips.

"And since the last place I want to spend tonight is in a Croatian prison, we need to get out of here." He pressed a quick, hard kiss to her mouth. "Right now."

"What about our drinks?" She gestured at the fancy fluted glasses sitting on the bar, sweating with condensation, completely forgotten in the heady rush of lust. She wondered idly how long they'd been sitting there, even as he grabbed her by the hand and pulled her away from them.

"I hate piña coladas."

She practically had to run to keep up with his long strides. "I don't," she teased, even though she was as desperate to get him naked as he was to let her.

"Then I'll order you as many as you want when we get back to my room."

"How far is it? Because my hotel is just over there and—"

He stopped to face her so abruptly that she almost slammed into his beautiful chest. "I packed my ties, Emma. All of them."

The look in his eyes set her world on fire.

"Your room it is."

* * * * *

COMING SOON!

We really hope you enjoyed reading this book. If you're looking for more romance, be sure to head to the shops when new books are available on

Thursday
23rd August

To see which titles are coming soon, please visit
millsandboon.co.uk

MILLS & BOON

LET'S TALK
Romance

For exclusive extracts, competitions
and special offers, find us online:

- facebook.com/millsandboon
- @millsandboonuk
- @millsandboon

Or get in touch on 0844 844 1351*

For all the latest titles coming soon, visit
millsandboon.co.uk/nextmonth